ALLEGIANCE UNRAVELS

BOOK 4 OF THE NATURE'S FURY SERIES

*An internal war wages when
duty conflicts with conscience*

A.E. FAULKNER

4700 Millenia Blvd.
Ste #175-90776
Orlando, FL 32839

info@indieowlpress.com
www.indieowlpress.com

ALLEGIANCE UNRAVELS

Cover design by Michelle Preast
Indie Book Cover Designs / Michelle-Preast.com

Interior layout by Vanessa Anderson
at NightOwlFreelance.com

Manufactured in the United States of America

Paperback ISBN-13: 978-1-949193-04-6

This book is dedicated to those who serve and sacrifice for others—you may never know how far-reaching your efforts span or how appreciated you truly are.

"We are not of what we feel or believe to do, we are of what
we do or fail to do."

— *Judith McNaught*

Contents

Contents

ALLEGIANCE UNRAVELS

BEFORE DARKNESS FELL

Chapter 1

"Change in plans," I announce, a moment after the "Call Ended" message flashes on my cell phone screen. My wife's narrowed eyes confirm that I'm stating the obvious. She huffs out a frustrated sigh and nods slightly, barely restraining her annoyance.

That quickly, our lazy Saturday afternoon, tinkering around the house, takes a sharp right turn. I'm accustomed to new assignments when my superior, Lieutenant Colonel Morris, deems it appropriate, so that part is easy to swallow. But this time, the location is a bit of a surprise. Instead of my usual commute to Fort Meade on Monday morning, I'll be heading to Langley Air Force Base in Virginia.

His only explanation is that he's been tasked to send his most capable logistics officer to serve on an urgent, critical project. I've dedicated two decades of my life to the U.S. military and I intend to serve until someone deems retirement necessary.

Lieutenant Colonel Morris said I was his number one choice when he received the request.

Pride brims within me. Of all the potential candidates that could fulfill that role, he chose me to represent our installation. And I am more than capable of meeting and exceeding whatever needs are presented.

I certainly don't mind my typical routine, but it's an honor to know that I've been called to serve this request. He didn't mention any others, so I assume I am the only one chosen.

One glance at my sullen wife deflates my ego. She's never thrilled when work takes me away for weeks or months at a time. *But this is what I signed up for.* As much as it annoys her when an unexpected request catches us off guard, Rossana knows that as well as I do.

I reach out and tug her hair. "Langley again. But it's only temporary. Two, maybe three, weeks." Her eyes crinkle slightly, and I know she's softening to the blow. Considering it could have been expected to last several months or more, a few weeks is tolerable. Riding on a potential wave of resolution, I blurt out, "Hey! Why don't you come with me? I'm sure there's plenty of wildlife you can photograph in Virginia. Maybe you can coax a smile out of a turtle or deer down there."

"What about Millie? Would she come with us?" Her eyes widen with hope. When she's happy, those green irises reflect a stunning shade of emerald. I will not be rewarded with that vision today.

"Certain breeds aren't allowed on base," I explain, cringing inwardly. We've had this conversation half a dozen times and it always ends the same way. I have no authority to question base policy, nor do I have the ability to change it.

Those eyes darken and narrow on me once more. I raise my hands in surrender. "Look, I don't agree with it and *I know* the only danger Millie poses is mauling people with her kisses, but that's the policy. We may not like it, but we have to abide by it."

She crosses her arms. "If she isn't welcome, then it's not the right place for me."

I nod, the brief surge of hopefulness crashing into disappointment. There's nothing else to say.

After a quiet dinner, I gather enough belongings for a week and neatly slip them into a duffel bag. I'm hopeful I won't need much more than that, but I can always launder uniforms on base if necessary. I make a point to pack my glasses in addition to contact lenses. I have a feeling I'll be putting in long days there, and these aging eyes will likely need some breaks. Hell, the look may give me an intellectual appearance when I'm meeting new peers and superiors.

Rossana wanders into the bedroom, plopping on the bed. "In the mood for a walk?" she asks.

I nod, gratefully accepting her peace offering. We leash Millie and trail behind her. Inhaling the fragrant late spring air, my eyes wander over the perfectly spaced houses lining our street. My senses absorb every sight and sound, mentally filing every detail so that I can recollect it when I'm drifting off to sleep alone in my room at the base. *I'll miss this.*

Chapter 2

Sunday passes in a blur of memories and moments. The three of us take a family trip to a local dog park. Rossana totes one of her smaller cameras, slipping the case's strap over her head. As we walk the perimeter, she snaps shots of Millie zooming around the open space. She loves the other dogs, and she's an "only child," so she curiously approaches any dog that expresses remote interest in her. Most dog owners are fine with it, able to see past her breed and grasp her non-threatening demeanor. But there's usually one that gives us the side eye, silently judging us and her. *How dare you bring a pit bull here?* Damn fools. She's better behaved than most of them anyway.

I savor the time, committing every laugh and smile to memory. Rossana sets the timer on her camera for a family photo. Even though Millie chooses that moment to drag her panting pink tongue over my cheek, it's the perfect shot. Rossana promises to send me the best of the day's pictures so I can scroll through them when I have a breather or whenever I'm counting down the days until I return home.

After dinner we relax on the couch before calling it an early night. Before we know it, dawn will break, and I'll need to get on the road.

My drive south is uneventful. I blend in with the rush hour traffic and pass some school busses here and there. School must be out soon. That means the kids living on base will be done soon too. More people running around with extra free time on their hands means one thing: more noise. Well, it will probably only be a week or so that I'm there. My office at Fort Meade keeps me pretty isolated, which suits me just fine.

After I park in the designated lot, I check my phone for new messages. As promised, Lieutenant Colonel Morris has emailed my tasking order, which includes specific reporting instructions.

After collecting a room key, my first stop is the officer's quarters. If this were a longer assignment and Rossana had come with me, we might have been assigned a house on the base, provided one was available. But since I came solo, and being that this is a temporary situation, I'm relegated to a dormitory-style room. Although, being a sergeant means that I'll be housed in quarters with other single officers and higher-ranking enlisted members. I'll have my own room, which suits me just fine. I'm not here to socialize. I'm here to kick this assignment's ass, impress my superiors, and return home.

I'm given a few hours to find my room and unpack my meager belongings. A few years ago, I visited this base for a long weekend. Thankfully, my memory and sense of direction still serve me well. I'll know my way around here in no time. Some of the buildings may have gotten a fresh splash of paint or structural upgrades, but the basic layout is similar enough that I can find the buildings I'll need—besides, most areas will fade into an irrelevant background. Since I'll only be here for a week or two, I plan to spend most waking moments immersed in work.

After a quick visit to the mess hall for lunch, I report to orientation. Six other uniform-clad soldiers surround the conference room table, all eager to understand why they've been summoned.

Captain Halak introduces himself and explains that we'll spend our time here preparing some logistical improvements to the base. We'll each leave this meeting with a list of tasks to fill our schedules for the rest of the week.

Then, next Monday, at 0900 hours, we'll meet with General David Kuraly. At that time, he will take the reins in overseeing this group.

I subtly shake my head in disbelief. *General David Kuraly.* I'd know that name anywhere. He is the highest ranking official on this base. He's responsible for the whole damn operation. I make a point of memorizing the names and ranks of leadership for any base where I'm stationed.

I silently wrestle my eyebrows to prevent them from revealing the surprise coursing through me. *The general? I'll be working directly with him?* Forcing myself to stay in the moment, I dismiss fantastical thoughts, such as dazzling my superior with my project management skills. *Must pay attention.*

By the end of the day, I'm clear on my assignment. Coordinate with an onsite facility point of contact to review the base's layout. Determine key locations that could accommodate additional buildings—temporary trailers really—that will function as offices. Then cross-reference military installations in the Midwest to determine if they are able to supply any of our needs. I'm instructed to avoid contacting bases along the East Coast, which makes no sense since some are fairly close. This would make for faster and cheaper shipping. But there must be a reason, so I don't question it. If all else fails, I will need to research and order new units, but that is not preferred.

So far, this assignment sounds like it's going to be as exciting as watching a hot air balloon inflate. It's just logistics: reviewing maps and shuffling inventory from one location to another. I'm certainly capable of completing these tasks, but it's disappointing, considering this was supposed to be "urgent and critical."

Chapter 3

The first week teems with tedium. I rise at dawn, grab breakfast at the chow hall, and sit in an office all day making phone calls or scouring military databases. I break for lunch, trekking again to the chow hall, before returning to the monotony that awaits me. Before the mess hall closes, I secure my last square meal of the day and return to my room. My reward for a long day of work is calling my wife. It's the last thing I do each night before my eyes close, before I wake up and repeat the motions all over again.

Rossana and I quickly settle into a routine and her mood seems to brighten with each passing day. *She probably thinks I'll be home soon. I have my doubts given that the days have consisted of busywork. It sounds like the meat of this assignment begins next week.* Nevertheless, hearing every last mundane detail of her day provides the exact escape I crave.

As a nature photographer, her days are spent largely isolated. Her regular companions include trees, bodies of water, and anything that may lurk or soar near them. She describes each day's location—sometimes it's a public garden, other days a wildlife refuge. She also regularly visits a local nature preserve and the mountains. She snaps pictures of hummingbirds, foxes, sunrises, and streams. If it moves, she'll take its photo.

I imagine the pride she feels when seeing one of her images on a calendar or magazine page rivals my own pride when I've successfully completed a mission. These days, my missions typically consist of pushing paperwork around on a desk or typing commands into a computer. No matter, my service is needed, and I will fulfill my duties as expected or beyond.

When the words subside, we say our goodbyes with the promise to speak again tomorrow. Only one task remains after I've showered and prepared to retire for the evening.

Whether I'm at our extended family's hunting cabin or deployed to an installation other than my home base, one constant companion lays in wait by my side when I sleep. I place the aircraft grade tactical flashlight on the nightstand. Its sleek black body contains a powerful burst of light that could easily immobilize a would-be intruder. When said intruder was disoriented, I could simply twist the flashlight in my palm and introduce the toothed bezel edge of the handle to his or her head.

Although I hope to never make use of it in such a way, I consider the tool an added layer of security when I'm at my most vulnerable somewhere other than home.

At the house, we've got Millie. And while she favors cuddles over aggression, she'll protect her humans if she perceives danger. I don't need a guard dog, though I do rely on her keen ears to alert me to unfamiliar noises before they reach a frequency I can detect. At home I can quickly access my hunting rifles if needed. The weapons that travel with me are much more portable.

Next, I retrieve my folding knife. The brown contoured handle reminds me of the inner rings of a tree, fanning wider as they stretch from the smooth center to the curved edges. Unsheathing it, I place the four-inch blade on the nightstand parallel to the tactical flashlight.

Although I don't anticipate handling a weapon this evening, or at any point while I'm here, I'll rest easier knowing that my safeguards are less than an arm's length away.

Folding down the crisp white sheets, I climb into bed and rest my head on the firm pillow. Anticipation for meeting the general threatens to keep my mind churning. Forcing my eyes closed, I patiently await sleep to overtake me.

The weekend is mostly uneventful, but I make an effort to fill the time. Unfortunately, spare moments allow my mind to drift to what I'd typically be doing at home. And I'd rather not dwell on that right now. Weather-permitting, Rossana and I would often treat Millie to an impromptu day trip to anywhere that the three of us can hike. From her constant travel, Rossana knows the most scenic, least populated spots to just relish the fresh air and enjoy nature.

After a revitalizing day, we'd return home for dinner. I'd

fire up the grill and even throw on an extra serving of steak or chicken for the dog.

I'd spend part of the weekend in my workshop, tinkering with whatever broken appliance had been deposited on my bench or just planning our next home improvement project.

Although it's tempting to drive home for the weekend, this isn't a commuting position. I'm on assignment and need to demonstrate my commitment. That means maintaining a presence on base until my mission is complete.

To maintain a healthy level of distraction, I explore the onsite fitness center. Taking advantage of the equipment at my disposal, I allow the weight room and an elliptical machine to monopolize most of my time before taking a jog on the treadmill.

Other than that minor excursion, I fill my time with work. Might as well complete as many tasks as possible if it'll get me home faster. While I'm in my temporary office, organizing paperwork for the new work week, a meeting notification chirps in my email. It's the official invitation to Monday morning's meeting with General Kuraly. The appointment subject is "High Priority Initiative." *I guess I'm not getting any more details about it now.*

By Sunday evening, I'm ready to tackle and complete the next work week. Besides, Monday morning should be interesting.

Chapter 4

Walking across base, I pass one of the streets lined with modest single-family homes. A woman, likely a soldier's spouse since she's not wearing fatigues, trails behind a leashed poodle. *Sure, that damn dog's allowed to live here but our pit bull's not allowed to step foot on the premises.*

I brush my frustration aside. Millie's a nervous wreck staying overnight anywhere but home anyway. As long as she's got her own bed and regular routine, she's pretty content. Besides, it's already been a week and I've made a serious dent in my to-do list. At this rate, I should be back home with my family next week. A gnawing in my gut cautions otherwise.

Quickening my pace, I continue to my destination: a conference room across campus. After studying maps of what must have been every inch of this base over the past few days, I could reach my destination in record time even if I was blindfolded.

Most of my time so far has consisted of plotting the placement of additional facilities and coordinating the delivery of temporary units. I'm not sure why the base needs additional offices in place so quickly. The only reason you'd need more buildings is to accommodate more people. *But this place doesn't appear to be bursting at the seams. What's this space needed for?* I guess I'll find out soon enough.

I choose the seat directly to the right of the head of the table. It's my subliminal method of being the leader's right-hand man. The polished cherry table reflects the harsh fluorescent lighting. Averting my eyes, I scan everyone in attendance. The other six soldiers from last week's orientation are here, as well as a few other faces I don't recognize. *Maybe they're located at this base permanently.* The orientation was probably just for the temporary transplants.

A slender soldier rushes into the room, gracefully sliding into a seat diagonal from mine. Her dark hair is pulled into a tight bun. Her serious eyes search the room, perhaps seeking a familiar face. She slips a stethoscope from her neck and gently rests it on the table. I've never seen her before. Which doesn't mean much since I haven't been here that long or ventured out to socialize or even paid much attention to those around me during mealtimes at the mess hall. This is a short-term assignment. I'm content to keep to myself, focusing on accomplishing tasks and rewarding a productive day with a call home.

I squint, attempting to force my aging eyes into focus so I can read her name badge. *These days I need my damn reading glasses to see anything.* N – O – O – something, something. Although she wears the standard-issue uniform, the stethoscope proclaims that she's a doctor or nurse. *Why the hell would she be here for this meeting? Since when is a medical professional needed at a strategy meeting?*

At precisely 0900 hours, General Kuraly arrives. His perfectly polished black shoes clack on the tile floor, echoing in the hushed space. His deep blue three-button coat swims in medals, ribbons, and badges. I knew the general was highly decorated, but I didn't expect the overwhelming dominance pervading his presence.

Everyone around the table rises, greeting the general and demonstrating their profound respect. When the general sits, we follow suit and he calls the meeting to order.

"Thank you all for joining me on short notice," he begins. "We've all got enough to do, and I'm about to increase your workload, so let's get right to the point. Two years ago, the Department of Operational Assets was formed with the responsibility of analyzing and recommending strategies to balance a rapidly growing population that conversely correlates with dwindling resources.

"I have been assigned to this operation since its inception. Under that umbrella, I developed the resources, infrastructure, and population arm of the initiative. At this point, the original team has completed its preliminary duties and, ready or not, the time has come for first phase implementation."

He rises from his seat, confidently pacing around the room. I sense that he's evaluating each one of us as he speaks. Forcing my eyes straight ahead, my heart jumps with each inflection as he emphasizes certain words. I don't dare look, but I'd bet his pale eyes trail up and down every soldier seated at this table. *Why do I suddenly feel like a rabbit being stalked by a wolf?*

Chapter 5

Lost in wandering thoughts, I refrain from shaking my head to refocus. I tune back to my surroundings in the midst of a dramatic pause. Thankfully, it lasts only a moment before the general continues. He clasps his hands behind his back, as if this is a casual conversation. "What does that have to do with us, you're probably asking yourselves."

Pivoting toward the table, he plunks a stubby finger down on the hard surface and answers. "Everything. Look around, people. Look into the eyes of everyone seated at this table." He pauses as we shift stunned gazes from him to each other. *This meeting is like no other I've ever attended.*

When all eyes return to him, General Kuraly shifts gears. "The topics we discuss in this room, among this group, stay right here. The only person you may discuss this project with outside of meetings is me. Is that clear?" It's technically a question, but the inflection of his tone commands an order. A chorus of "Yes, sir" echoes through the room.

With that, he nods proudly.

Of course, we all gave the right answer. Who wouldn't?

He returns to his seat and rests his outstretched hands on the table, gently tapping his fingers on the surface as he speaks. His pale blue eyes travel the room, as if ensuring he holds the rapt attention of his audience.

He explains that this Department of Operational Assets developed recommendations that were under review. None were ready to be deployed, but an upcoming circumstance is going to present an opportunity to test some of the proposed strategies before they're implemented large-scale.

Silent skepticism permeates the room. We're basically a logistics team with a set plan to follow. *Give me a clipboard and a checklist and I'll get it done.* Maybe I can finish my part sooner rather than later and get the hell home.

The general shuffles papers around the table, motioning for each of us to take one. My eyes sweep over the words, noting certain phrases. *Opening bases for short-term public occupancy. Monitoring food supplies. Tracking civilian population pockets.*

None of this sounds right. *We're not in the business of babysitting civilians.* I glance around the table. In a less-controlled environment, these people would probably be narrowing their eyes and scrunching up their faces in disbelief. In the general's presence, blank expressions remain fixed on paper, impartial eyes sliding across printed words.

This whole scenario sends warning jolts up my spine. It's probably just the intimidation oozing from the presence of such a high ranking official. For now, I'll chalk it up to the cumulative discomfort of a new situation, a temporary peer group, and an assignment that's about to skyrocket in importance.

"General," a clipped, accented voice begins. "I do not understand what possible role I could play in this plan." It's the doctor. Or nurse. The woman with the stethoscope.

Kuraly's ice cold irises shift to her. "Dr. Noori, trust me, your input will play a crucial role in this strategy. There is a… biochemical component that you will lead." A hint of confusion mars her dark features. After just a second of hesitation, she acknowledges his vague answer.

"Yes, sir," she acquiesces, shifting her gaze back to the paper in her hands.

I imagine she's thinking the same thing I'm thinking. *What the hell is he not telling us?*

Before the meeting ends, pounding erupts behind my temples. The general dismisses us after providing a stern reminder that the team's tasks will remain confidential. To highlight the importance of this initiative, he informs us that we will reconvene tomorrow and each day after until we've made significant progress.

I move through the appropriate motions for the rest of the day, mindlessly carrying out duties. My thoughts drift back to Kuraly's words. The government's predictive models indicate that we are on the cusp of demand exceeding supply when it comes to basic resources: food, fuel, clean water, and clean air. And the solution is to better manage the population.

There was no mention of businesses working to reduce emissions and pollution. Or that corporate America is discovering new ways to recycle, reuse, and reduce waste. Or that food manufacturers are striving to deliver affordable, healthy options that rely on renewable plant sources. *So instead of putting long term processes into place before or within the food supply process, we're making changes at the end consumer level?* Sounds ass-backward to me but I'll just keep that thought to myself. I must be missing some critical components, and today's information overload leaves my brain too exhausted to further analyze the newly acquired information.

According to the general, this initiative has been fast-tracked due to an impending event that will allow us to pilot test the recommended strategies. Tomorrow we'll be fully briefed. In the meantime, the non-transplants have been ordered to offload about half of their current work. Those of us who were called from other bases have no other assignment, so it's not a problem for us.

This way, the burden is lessened for those already on base. Other team members can still assist with their usual work, but less manpower is needed since our group of transplants will tackle this initiative's tasks full-time. The balance will allow maximum focus on assignments without drawing too much attention to the pilot test. The general assures us that everyone in residence at this installation will be impacted by the changes to come and there is a plan in place to deploy communications to all base personnel. It's not our place to share that information beforehand.

The level of secrecy sends a ripple of alarm through me. We're all trained military soldiers and with that comes a level of self-control and maturity that should not require multiple reminders to maintain confidentiality. *What exactly are we hiding?*

Chapter 6

Keeping to myself throughout the day, I continue to chip away at the preliminary tasks assigned to me last week. When my eyes need a break from the reports, emails, and research, I allow them to drift to the only personal item in this office: a framed photo of Rossana and Millie. Their *presence* serves as a brief respite from the mundane.

I break only to grab quick meals in the mess hall before retiring to my room for the evening. My nightly call home goes much the same as every other night. Rossana answers with hope for news that my assignment is ending soon.

Attempting to diffuse the pride swelling as I recount the level of importance General Kuraly deemed this initiative, I admit that the team stands at the threshold of a looming task list. Although I don't know exactly what I'll be doing yet, I have a feeling a heap of work awaits. At least the general's urgency may benefit me here. I'm fine focusing all of my free time fulfilling duties. I assume all the transplants will return to their home base when the mission is complete.

News that the urgent project I've been recruited to work on has barely begun deflates Rossana's hope, and mood, instantly. Desperate to change the subject, I ask about what I'm missing at home. Unfortunately, that isn't the best topic either.

"So, you know Greg's work truck?"

"Yeah," I confirm. The neighbor across the street works for a pest control company. He drives a company truck home, so it's parked in his driveway on nights and weekends.

"He must have had a hole in the drum or something. Chemicals leaked from it and ran right into the stream," she explains. "Whatever was in there turned the water murky and pretty much killed anything living in it."

The stream runs behind Greg's house and through a concrete tunnel beneath the road. It borders our yard, flowing beyond, into a wooded area that separates us from the next lot.

"Oh geez," I sigh. Tapping into her experiences coaxing wildlife into a comfortable lull, at least long enough to snap a few photos, she's managed to make our backyard a small haven for the local deer, rabbits, squirrels, and birds. Besides the fifty-pound bags of corn she spreads along the wooded edges of our property, the stream has always been a magnet for creatures of the two-and-four-legged variety.

"He contacted the township and they're sending someone out to look at it, but what can they really do?" she asks. "The damage is done."

I rub my temples. The pounding has returned. "That takes

years to clear up," I mutter. "I'm guessing you won't find any subjects to photograph there for a while." Then, in an effort to block thoughts of what I can't change, I ask, "Did you take any pictures today?"

"Yeah," she says, seemingly distracted. "I drove to Catoctin. Took Millie along for the ride. We hiked and I got some shots of the mountain ridge."

Now that's exactly what the doctor ordered. I ask enough questions that she finally gives up answering and instead offers a detailed account of her day.

The words play like a movie reel in my mind. I can almost feel the humid air clinging to my skin and the sun's rays peeking through the canopy of oak, hickory, and maple trees. I allow my mind the luxury of indulging itself in her rich descriptions. And I always have the photos to look forward to. Even though I'm not present for most of her shoots, just feasting my eyes upon the stunning images she captures instantly transports me behind the lens, to the exact moment she caught faster than the blink of an eye.

By the time she finishes, the stress of my day has dissipated. A hot shower diffuses any lingering tension and I prepare for a restful sleep. Today was overwhelming. Just meeting the general was an undertaking. His imposing presence both commands and swallows a whole room.

Still, I'm intrigued. Whatever this is exactly, it's important. And only a select few have been called to the table. No matter what tomorrow brings, I will be ready for the challenge. I am part of this team for a reason and I look forward to a new day of helping my team succeed.

Positioning my flashlight and knife on the nightstand, I switch the lights off and allow my mind and body the opportunity to recharge.

Chapter 7

Waking with the sunrise, I start the new day ready to jumpstart my tasks. Any uncertainty or discomfort I felt yesterday was probably just jumbled nerves. I'm away from my home base, as well as my family, working with people I've just met. There's been small talk among the transplants who've been here just over a week now, but it's nothing like the comfortable camaraderie that naturally develops with those you've worked with for years.

The more I learn about this initiative, the more sense it will make, and the less unsettled I'll feel. With a renewed focus, I grab a quick breakfast and dig into the awaiting pile of paperwork on my temporary desk. Keeping one eye on the clock, I'm able to cross off a few items on my to-do list before today's meeting with the general.

Allowing myself twenty minutes to walk the short distance to the conference room, I arrive in plenty of time for the meeting. And plenty of time to claim my preferred seat—directly to the right of the head of the table. The others trickle in within a few minutes. No one would dare be late. Silence and anticipation charge the air. The faces and names run together, but it appears we have full attendance prior to the general's arrival.

Punctuality is a characteristic I appreciate. If I got a dollar for every time my wife was punctual, I'd be quite strapped for cash. I allow thoughts of home to creep through my mind because they serve as motivation to complete this assignment.

About two minutes before our slated start time, the clack of General Kuraly's stiff shoes echoes in the hallway. The group collectively straightens, squares shoulders, tugs shirt hems down, and brushes away real or imaginary lint.

With a sharp nod, the general greets us and takes his seat at the head of the table. Captain Halak trails behind him and selects a seat along the wall, a seemingly casual observer. Another soldier follows, planting herself next to Halak. She's a captain too— easily identifiable by the rank insignia on her uniform.

With no introduction of this newcomer and no time for niceties, Kuraly jumps right into our purpose.

"As I explained yesterday, this group is embarking on a project that will help ensure the long-term viability of our great nation's resources. Each of you is a cog in this plan," he begins. *Well that's a new one. Never been called that before.*

"We function together, or we cease to progress." Splaying his thick fingers on the table's shiny surface, he pushes back in the chair and rises. *Can't this guy sit still? I hope I've got that much energy when I'm his age.*

"I've explained how our combined efforts will support this mission. In order to move forward, we'll break into smaller, strategically focused groups. You will still have individual assignments, but the other members of your group will depend on you to advance with your duties so that they can advance with theirs. Some of you will be assigned to work directly with two of my commanding officers." He nods to Captain Halak and the soldier sitting next to him. "They will help ensure that you stay on track and meet expected deadlines. This will allow us all to work more efficiently and accomplish the tasks within our multiple roles simultaneously. You will be grouped with those you will work most closely with, although you may find yourself reaching out to others on the team on occasion. I ask that you remember how imperative it is that we remain confidential in the information we share outside of this room. Discussions regarding this initiative may only be discussed with your commanding officer or each other."

He pauses, peering around the table. We're all fixated on him, just like we've been since he crossed the threshold of the conference room. The urge to squirm in my seat overwhelms every nerve when his focus zeroes in on me. Thankfully, it only hovers there for a moment before it shifts to the doctor. A slight smile crosses his face when he singles out two of those within our ranks.

"Sergeant Bowen and Dr. Noori will work directly with me."

I've made a significant effort to maintain a positive attitude toward this assignment. But hearing my name called in this capacity sends a nervous flash through my core. Of course, it's everything I wanted: acknowledgement from the general and the chance to impress him. *How can progress toward my overall goal here invoke such an unsettling feeling?*

After doling out assignees to their designated commanding officers, Kuraly ensures that everyone is confident in their purpose. With no opposing statements, he dismisses the subgroups so that their work can begin.

When the room stands silent, occupied by just me, Dr. Noori, and the general, he promptly addresses us, "I'll be working with the two of you directly because you're being entrusted with the most critical roles in this mission and they are interrelated. You will complete your components individually, but they will be deployed on a tiered implementation, each task relying and building upon the one before it."

Intrigue and pride whisper in the back of my mind. *Most critical roles.*

"We'll discuss next steps in my office. Follow me." With that, he turns on his heel and strides out the door. I beckon for Dr. Noori to go before me. She nods in appreciation then slows her pace, so we trail behind the general together.

Chapter 8

The three of us relocate to General Kuraly's office, which is housed in the same building. Unlocking and swinging the door open, he motions for us to sit, sweeping an arm toward the burgundy leather chairs opposite his monstrous desk.

The doctor and I settle into seats while Kuraly lowers himself into his. He slides a labeled pile of manila folders toward each of us. The genuine smile on his face signals that he's pleased to literally push this work off on us. Or perhaps it's pride in the project he's leading.

Either way, I grab the stack before me. The sooner I get started, the sooner I finish. And demonstrating enthusiasm for the task at hand certainly won't hurt. Dr. Noori eyes hers cautiously before casting a perplexed gaze at the general.

Clasping his hands together, Kuraly leans forward, resting his elbows on the desk.

"Now, the real work begins," he starts. "It's going to take a full team to complete this mission, but just between us, you two are the heavy-hitters. You're going to operationalize this mission. We have two weeks before we hit the ground running, so to speak."

Leaning toward me, he explains. "Sergeant, your first task is to prepare this base for an influx of people. We'll need security measures put into place, temporary intake offices set up, and we will need to alter housing assignments. I'd prefer to keep the evacuees grouped together while minimizing inconvenience to our personnel."

"Yes, sir," I nod, forcing a stoic mask to permeate my features while an inner voice screams that this request is impossible. While I have spent the past week securing temporary offices, coordinating delivery, and planning their placement on base, that's just one layer of this onion. I need to beef up security, furnish the new offices, and reassign living quarters. And that's just the start of a mission that must be completed in two weeks. *Sure, maybe I can lay out a football field in that time as well, just for kicks.*

Perhaps assuming I'm confident in accomplishing all he's asked, the general turns his attention to Dr. Noori. Her posture and appearance exhibit attentiveness.

"Doctor, your files contain formulas for a serum that's been in development for the past two years. Minimal testing has been conducted on the serum's…effectiveness. And that's where you come in. I need you to review the work that's already been done and verify that every 't' has been crossed and every 'i' has been dotted."

Dr. Noori hangs on his every word, radiating confidence.

This is probably a walk in the park for her. While she's checking and double-checking someone else's work, I'll be drowning in logistical details. Kuraly must sense her aptitude for this assignment. He continues.

"Then I'll need you to test the serum to ensure it does exactly what we want it to do. After you've completed that step, we'll need to mass produce the final product. We will mobilize it as an injectable vaccine." The smirk spreading across his pale cheeks confirms the pride this initiative brings him.

"Sir, what sort of quantities are we aiming for?" the doctor asks. "Should I prepare any of my staff to assist with this process?" The smirk drops from Kuraly's face and he points to the stack of manila folders resting between the two of them.

"Dr. Noori, while it is imperative that as few people as possible know about this right now, I will allow you to assemble a small team when the work necessitates it. For now, refer to your folders. You'll find answers to many of your questions in there." As if suddenly remembering that I'm here too, he adds, "Both of you. Bring yourselves up to speed on what has been done already by reviewing the information I've provided."

Folding his hands and resting his elbows on the smooth mahogany surface, the general leans forward.

"Sergeant Bowen, I understand that you've put the wheels in motion for securing temporary units that can be used as additional office space. Is that correct?"

"Yes, sir." Before I can provide any details such as the number of units and where they'll be positioned on base, he continues.

"Good." He narrows his eyes in thought. "When those units arrive, alert me if you need another member of the team to assist with the logistics. That part may be better suited to someone who resides on base." I nod in appreciation, grateful for even the possibility of unloading some of my workload.

Pushing away from his high-backed chair, he rises. "Review your files and report back here at 0900 hours in the morning. We'll discuss the next phase of your assignment at that time."

Dr. Noori and I part ways and return to our respective offices. I spend the rest of the day poring through page after page of strategies and recommendations. This initiative was clearly meant for wide-scale implementation over the course of several years. And now we're expected to deploy it—granted, on a much smaller scale—in just two weeks' time.

As I absorb each section, each paragraph, and each word, a throbbing ache ignites behind my temples. It grows stronger with every hour that passes. By late afternoon, my stiff muscles demand movement. I pack up the unread files among the stack Kuraly gave me and lock the office door before I pull it closed for the day.

Chapter 9

Collecting a tray of tonight's featured meal: turkey, gravy, mashed potatoes, and mixed vegetables, I locate an empty table toward the back of the mess hall and claim it. Someone kindly left behind a copy of the base newspaper. *That'll make good company.*

I slide it across the table. Heeding the plea of my tired eyes, I merely skim the photos and headlines while loading my fork with potatoes. Although I've read about a lifetime's worth of words today, dining with a distraction absolves me from appearing antisocial. I'm perfectly content to eat alone. The paper further supports that image by guiding my focus downward, allowing me to avoid awkward eye contact with other diners that I may, but very likely don't, know.

Voices and footsteps fade into the background as I breeze over the day's news—a reminder of tomorrow's free health screenings, notice of leagues forming at the on-base bowling alley, and an end-of-school-year celebration at the on-base school.

For a few moments I savor the solitude. All too soon a shadow falls over my refuge. I count to thirty, hoping it passes. When it doesn't budge, I slide my tired eyes upward.

Dr. Noori stands before me, eyebrows raised expectantly. A few wisps of dark hair stray from the tight bun pulled at the nape of her neck. Her deep brown eyes evaluate my reaction, which I attempt to keep neutral. She tilts her head toward a chair and asks, "May I join you?"

I'd really rather she didn't. "Of course," I concede, folding the newspaper into quarters. She slides her thin frame into the chair across from me. *Okay, now what?*

"So, I assume you are keeping busy with the new assignment," she says quietly, pushing corn and carrot bits around on her plate. *She knows we're not supposed to be talking about this. And small talk is a waste of time.*

"That I am," I confirm. When she doesn't respond, I feel compelled to reciprocate the question. "And you?" *I'm not one for treading on thin ice and I fear that's exactly her plan.*

A combination of fear and relief flashes through her serious gaze and her shoulders visibly relax. *Bingo. That's what she was waiting for—an invitation to talk about the one thing we aren't supposed to talk about.*

"Yes, it has been *challenging*," she stresses the last word, maintaining eye contact. "The more I learn about what I am supposed to be doing, the more concerned I become that I don't agree with all of it."

Suppressing muscles that are aching to twitch, I stifle the instinct to raise my palms in a "Stop right there" motion. Instead, I verbally attempt to halt this line of conversation.

"Well, I see it as a mission to complete and I have no plans to shirk my duties," I simply state, shifting my eyes to the mound of mashed potatoes bordering the turkey. Shoveling a forkful of each, held together with a healthy dollop of gravy, I dive into my dinner. If this discussion continues, I may end up cutting mealtime short and retreating to my room. If that happens, I'll be hitting the vending machines tonight for sustenance.

With a renewed motivation, I focus on emptying my plate. The doctor takes the hint.

"I apologize," she states. "I did not mean to make you uncomfortable. I simply thought we were in the same boat… as they say." She slides her chair back and rises. "Good evening, Sergeant," she says as she grasps her tray and excuses herself.

Eyeing the newspaper wistfully, I leave it untouched. I eat as quickly as possible without compromising basic manners and hustle back to my room. It's been a long day and the only thing left to look forward to is calling home.

"You sound tired." *Ah, that wife of mine is perceptive.*

"I am," I admit. "I've got a ton of information to pore through before a meeting in the morning."

"Well, we can keep our call short then," she offers. Great, the best part of my day finally arrives and it's about to be curtailed. She's right, though. I've got a few more hours' worth of pages to review and notes to make and bedtime can't come fast enough tonight.

After a smattering of small talk, we end the conversation. I promise to be a better conversationalist tomorrow evening. I neglect to mention the general's plan to deploy this initiative in two weeks. Although I didn't confirm, I have a sneaking suspicion that my presence will be required well beyond those two weeks. We've had enough of a damper on our evening.

Chapter 10

Dr. Noori and I both arrive at General Kuraly's office a solid ten minutes before our scheduled debriefing at 0900 hours. I greet her with a curt nod. I'm tempted to ask if she's done her homework, meaning read her share of the files we were given yesterday. But I don't want to encourage conversation about this forbidden topic, even if it's meant in jest.

The general summons us in at the top of the hour. We both stride toward the seats we occupied yesterday. Once we're settled, he launches into the meeting.

"I trust you both reviewed the information I provided to you yesterday."

We both proclaim an affirmative, "Yes, sir."

"Good." Resting his elbows on the desk, he steeples his fingers. "I'd like each of you to provide me with a summary of your priorities. This is also an opportunity for you to ask any questions you have at this point."

Damn. I'm glad I burned the midnight oil last night and read every last word on each page provided to me.

Kuraly's smile slides into a near-sneer. "Ladies first, Dr. Noori."

My ears perk with these words. While I have a good handle on my role in this initiative, I'm curious to understand how our work will intersect. I'm also wondering what aspects of this assignment she doesn't agree with, and whether she'll bring it to the general's attention.

The doctor explains that she's reviewed all of the documentation and that her primary directive is to create an injectable serum that will host a nano-tech tracker. She acknowledges that the technology portion has already been developed. Now the serum must be perfected. Her predecessors developed formulas, but they hadn't finalized which would best serve their needs. She's confident she can replicate the serum varieties to determine which would prove optimal, but she'll need to order some supplies as well as chemicals. My mind drifts when she launches into an explanation about proteins and antibodies, but Kuraly listens intently.

When she questions if any of her staff can assist with this process, the general raises three stubby fingers in the air. "Three. You determine three members of your medical team who can be trusted to maintain confidentiality. You will share no details of the project during your briefings with them. All they need to know is what duties to carry out and the timeline for their tasks."

"Yes, sir," Dr. Noori agrees.

Resting his hands on the desk, he takes her acquiescence as a cue to continue. "Even though our group is breaking out into individualized assignments, it does not mean that we can become lax about the confidential status of this initiative. If you absolutely require further assistance at the point of mass production, we'll talk again at that time. Until then, I trust you can manage the resources I'm allowing to meet the requirements to make this mission a success."

It's clearly a command, not up for discussion. Dr. Noori acknowledges his statement with an affirmative, "Yes, sir."

The general grants Dr. Noori sweeping approval to purchase whatever equipment or supplies needed. She assures him that she will complete the final steps in preparing a serum as soon as the necessary materials arrive.

She confirms that the ultimate goal is to develop a single-injection syringe containing a substance that carries and deposits the tracking device into the body. Each device must be assigned to an individual and recorded so that the individual becomes "tagged" with an identification number.

And this is where the overlap occurs. While she oversees syringe production, my job is to mobilize it. I must ensure that we have a system in place to record identification numbers as well as to monitor those numbers, so we can see the recipients' location at any time.

Dr. Noori opens and closes her mouth, momentarily hesitating. Straightening the papers within her folder, she inhales a deep breath and finds her voice.

"Sir, I don't understand who is going to allow us to do this… to inject them with a tracking device. I assume a small portion of people would willingly accept it, but I tend to believe most would not. And in that sense, I question the need for mass production."

For just a flicker of a moment, Kuraly's eyes widen. He instantly recovers from any surprise her question triggered. I don't know my coworker very well, but it's obvious she's sharp. And thorough. I'm guessing those are the very qualities needed to complete an assignment like this.

But based on our superior's reaction, I'm also guessing this was one of the last things she should have vocalized in this moment.

The general presses both palms flat against the desk, conveying a thoughtful posture. "Dr. Noori, I assure you that the information provided to us is meant for immediate deployment. This project has already been approved at the highest level and it is not within our jurisdiction to question it."

I doubt there's much of anything out of his jurisdiction, so he must mean hers. And mine by association.

"Is there anyone who worked on this project that I should contact if I have any questions about the data and notes provided, sir? If I run into any stumbling blocks, it could greatly help my progress."

She's relentless. I'll give her that.

Kuraly smiles, but a hint of condescension lingers in it. "There's no need for that. I have been assured that everything you need is right here." He pats the stack of folders before her, holding her gaze.

"Thank you, sir." She reclines back into the chair slightly. The movement radiates defeat, though, not simply shifting into a more comfortable position.

At least she knows when to finally quit.

Perhaps in response to this exchange, the general takes a

moment to reinforce our understanding of the situation. He explains that this is part of a much bigger initiative, coming straight from the top. The ultimate purpose is to manage the population, monitoring pockets in case the government needs to step in and distribute resources in a balanced manner.

Why now? What isn't he telling us? Of course I don't question my superior. Besides, I'm pretty sure the doctor already ruffled his feathers enough for one day.

Regardless of the specific assignment, my job as both a sergeant and a soldier is to grasp the information provided to me and act upon it to fulfill my role in a satisfactory manner. And that's exactly what I'll do. I haven't been asked for input on the strategy. That's up to my superiors, although maybe someday soon I'll be part of a team developing long-term initiatives that will strengthen the future prosperity of our country.

When asked to summarize my role, I respond with an overview: develop an online system that generates unique tracking numbers associated with each injection, ensure that system captures demographic data from civilians entering the base, and create a needs assessment of the human and equipment resources each new intake office will require to process an influx of temporary guests.

This time a genuine smile spreads across the general's face. He appreciates my brevity and lack of any challenge to the process.

"Sergeant, whatever you come up with will eventually be shared across all bases nationwide," Kuraly continues. "Reach out to Chara in the I.T. Department. He's the Division Information Officer and he is aware that the program you're working on will require technological expertise to succeed. He's been instructed to clear his schedule when you make contact."

My trusted lined notebook and pen aren't going to cut it this time. I definitely need assistance when it comes to creating a computer program. Relief swells in my chest at the thought of sharing some of this workload with someone else.

"Yes, sir." *It sounds like I need to figure this out ASAP.*

"Oh, and Sergeant, I'd like you to align this with Census data," Kuraly adds. "It's our most comprehensive body of population statistics and it will perfectly complement our needs. Chara can help you with that too. Be sure to mention it."

Without asking if we have any further questions or concerns, Kuraly dismisses us both.

Chapter 11

Before anyone can stop me, I rush out the door and stride back to my room. Details, alternating with vague instructions, swirl in my mind. The best way to block them for a short time is by calling home. I deposit the manila files on the dorm-room-sized desk, knowing this respite will be brief. After a quick meal, I'll review every paper, chart, and reference that's been provided to me. Again. I hit a homerun during today's meeting with the general and I don't intend to compromise my batting average.

Relief surges when Rossana answers on the second ring. We bypass the niceties and delve into her day. Besides not wanting to bore her with mundane details of my schedule, I technically shouldn't share anything about my current assignment. Plus, her work is much more interesting than mine. Many times, I've envisioned her photoshoot locations, painting images in my mind from her vivid descriptions. Unfortunately, that escape is not meant to come today.

"I drove all the way out to Black Rock Cliff today. It was the perfect day for a hike. I got there just before dawn."

"Right," I interject. "You've shot there probably a dozen times before. Seems like it's always a good choice to see foxes and deer. And, of course, the amazing views."

"Not today," she sighs. "I didn't see one animal out in the open long enough to snap a photo. Not one." *That's odd.* She's always had success there. I can't even count how many photos she's shown me from that one location.

"And not only that, but I noticed the leaves are thinning out. I bet if I compared today's landscape shots to photos I took last year it would show that the trees are starting to look skimpy. It's way too early for the leaves to drop."

Knowing her, she'll spend hours tonight combing through her collections to compare the photos she took today to ones from previous trips. At least I know she's keeping busy while we're apart.

"It's just so strange," she elaborates. "It's like they know something we don't and they're going into hiding. The most I saw were some tail-ends scurrying away. And I didn't even have Millie with me to warn them that the camera was coming out."

"I bet you'll have better luck next time," I offer. "It was just a fluke. Or maybe you needed Millie with you, as a good luck charm."

"Maybe." Her voice sounds distant, as if she's still at Black Rock Cliff, searching for sentient life among the trees, brush, and trails. "So, how was your day? Did you pass your test?"

"Test? What test?" *Has one odd morning pushed her off the deep end?*

"Well, last night you were really tired, but you had to study some information. It just reminded me of preparing for an exam. You know, staying up all night to cram?"

"Oooohhh." *I wish it were that simple.* "As a matter of fact, today is shaping up to be a pretty good day. I met with the general and I think he was impressed."

"That's great!" Her genuine happiness for me slices through the disappointment that weighed down her failed photo shoot. "Maybe he'll reward you by sending you home soon!" she gushes. *At least she's got a sense of humor about this.*

"I fear it's just the opposite," I admit. "But my plan is to complete this assignment with flying colors so they can send me on my way."

"I'll drink to that," she says. The smile playing across her lips resonates in her words. At least our conversation has lifted her mood. Just hearing that familiar voice sends a wave of comfort through me. No matter what happens here, it's all temporary. And there's much to look forward to when I return home.

When our conversation ends, I hike to the mess hall, grab some grub, and then march back to the office to put in a few more hours of work. I bypass an evening call to Rossana since we talked already. My evening consists of studying, mapping out tasks, and memorizing details. Before I know it, my heavy eyes lure me to an early slumber.

Morning arrives, but instead of waking refreshed, my brain craves solitary confinement. It's processed way too much information in the past 48 hours. What I wouldn't give to tinker around in my workshop back home for the day—the power tools are probably already coated in a layer of dust from disuse.

It is not to be. This assignment isn't going anywhere, so neither am I. In making contact with the I.T. guy, Chara, yesterday, he asked that I review some reports before we officially convene. He said he'd print them and place them in an envelope at the front desk in his building. So that is my first stop today—after refueling.

I grab a quick breakfast in the mess hall and wash it down with a bitter cup of black coffee. If I swing by Chara's building on the way to my office, I can get started reviewing his data right away. My eyes can't wait to peruse through more stacks of paper.

Locating his building is no problem: it's the same one that houses General Kuraly's office. I glide through the front doors and locate a thick manila envelope with my name on it at the front reception area.

I've got my priority for today. Once I've digested this information, my strategy meetings with Chara will begin. I know what needs to be done to accomplish this mission. His technological capabilities will maximize our speed and efficiency in the process.

With the folder in hand, I turn on my heel and stride toward the entrance. The clack of stiff shoes echoes on the tile. Plenty of early birds on a military base. Technically, the base never closes. This mini-city operates all hours, seven days a week, and it takes many hands to function smoothly.

Just as I'm about to cross the threshold leading me back outside, a deep voice stops me in my tracks. I'd recognize it anywhere.

"Bowen, just the person I wanted to see." I comprehend the combination of letters and sounds but the statement is surreal. The person in charge of this whole base is looking for me.

With my shoulders back and chin raised, I turn to face General Kuraly. He smiles, meeting my eyes. No sense of warmth emanates from his greeting, but I don't require that from a superior. I imagine it takes a level of emotional distance to rise to a certain level of leadership. No matter. I smile and nod, ready to serve in whatever capacity is needed.

"Yes, sir."

"Do you have a few minutes? I was hoping we could talk in my office."

Well, seeing how his office is just down the hallway, and there's no chance in hell I'd refuse a request he made, my response is redundant. "Yes, sir."

Chapter 12

The walk to his office is short and silent. The general doesn't appear to waste time on small talk. Anticipation fuels each step I take. He unlocks the door and sweeps it open.

Dropping the keys in a drawer, he motions with his hand. "Take a seat, Sergeant." Sliding a rich leather chair back a foot, I lower myself into it. The firm cushion and perfectly polished wooden arms don't appear to get much use. But here I am, readying for a one-on-one meeting with none other than General David Kuraly.

As he settles into his large chair, I allow a few seconds to marvel at the fact that I'm back in the same seat I occupied less than twenty-four hours ago.

Straightening in the armchair, I lean slightly forward, subtly conveying my complete interest in this impromptu meeting. His icy eyes graze over me. Calculating, evaluating me from where he sits behind the monstrous mahogany desk. "You know, I like to think of you as my right-hand man."

Well damn. My subliminal seat choice at meetings must have worked.

"Yes, sir." Pride washes away any lingering doubts I may have had about this initiative and the general's intentions.

"You may have noticed that your assignment on this project began the moment you stepped on base."

"Yes, sir." *I sound like a damn record on repeat. He's probably used to that, though.*

He watches for a reaction, but he should know better than anyone that I've been trained to remain stoic and unreadable. A small smirk tugs on the corners of his lips: pride. Maybe I just confirmed that he chose the right person for the job.

Now it's my turn to let pride swell within. Maybe a promotion sits on the other end of this assignment. If I can exceed his expectations, it could mean a higher rank. And the faster I can finish my work here, the sooner I can get home.

He steeples his fingers, peering over them at me. "I had an idea that I'd like you to pursue. I know you're developing a software program that will address the tracking component. But if something went wrong and we were unable to retrieve data, we could be out of luck. I think we need a fail-safe. Something to help ensure our success."

"What did you have in mind, sir?" While I see the value in his thought process, this is going to translate into more work. And more work means more time to complete it.

"Wearable technology—like smart phones, smart watches, fitness trackers." He plants a pointer finger on the desk, accentuating his point. "I'd like you and Chara to explore incorporating existing technology into our computer program. Basically, if it's got a GPS within it, and it's a personal device, just think about how much that would improve our level of tracking accuracy. If we can somehow tie that in with the data we collect at the point of civilian intake, that would be our fail-safe."

I must be misinterpreting his request. Because if he's suggesting what I'm taking from his word choice, then I'd assume there are privacy laws we'd be breaking, or perhaps bending.

"So we would ask entrants to provide phone numbers and access to their fitness trackers upon intake, sir? As a field within the registration information we collect?" I verify. Not everyone even has those items, so it could not be required information. And what if they did have said devices but refused to share details about them? *Hell, I would hesitate to provide that sort of access to my personal information.*

He releases a sigh and his eyes narrow momentarily. Disappointment lurks in his features. *How the hell did this conversation plummet so quickly?* The wave of pride from our initial conversation has receded.

"Sergeant, asking for that information voluntarily could too easily result in erroneous information—by means of human error in data entry and the human tendency to lie when asked to provide information one would rather not share. Although I understand why you would suggest it, the concept diminishes our accuracy and allows for refusal."

He leans forward, resting his elbows on the desk. He's clearly worked out the need for this in his brain and I don't believe he's inviting feedback.

"I'd like for you and Chara to determine a way to connect that information to our data instantaneously. Then, at the point of intake, we would be secure in knowing that we've done everything possible to ensure we can track these people. We'd just be employing back-up techniques to help us negate any potential margin of error in Dr. Noori's work."

Although I barely know her, I have no doubts in the doctor's abilities. Her persona embraces intelligence, sincerity, and reliability. Masking my confusion, I hesitate to respond. I have no place questioning the general's request. *I've already seen how unsuccessful that can be.*

"Look, Sergeant," Kuraly starts, raising his palms as if placating me. "I don't mean to imply that I'm questioning Dr. Noori's competence. I'm just acknowledging that she was handed someone else's work to finish and in record time. That certainly increases the margin for error for anyone in that position."

That makes a lot of sense. I can only hope he's that understanding of me if there's anything he's assigned that I'm unable to accomplish in the expedited timeframe.

I suddenly understand Dr. Noori's subtle protests yesterday. The more I learn about this assignment, the more there is to question.

Chapter 13

As I nod in understanding, the general's desk phone rings. Swiveling his chair toward the left side of the desk, Kuraly mutters under his breath, "I'll send this to voicemail." But when his eyes drop to the phone's display, his expression shifts from annoyance to surprise in seconds. Raising a pointer finger, he distractedly says, "Excuse me. I've got to take this."

He raises the receiver and promptly answers, "Good morning, sir."

I wonder who that is. Who does the highest-ranking person on this base call "sir?" I get the answer rather quickly. Although I can only hear one side of the conversation, Kuraly is clearly trying to placate the caller.

"President Taves, I assure you that we will meet our deadline." The general's icy blue eyes wash over me, silently conveying my duty to fulfill his promise. I hold my posture and expression, unwilling to show the nerves rattling through every muscle in my body.

The general's talking to the president. The President of the United States. And my assumption, from the conversation tidbits that float to my ears, is that I'm part of the project they're discussing. He's genuinely interested in *my* work.

I slide a palm over my chin, attempting to mask the pride seeping through a subtle smile.

"I know, sir, and we're on target to deploy the serum before the…deadline." He stares at me, as if that will magically enable this deadline to be met.

When the rushed conversation concludes, he returns the phone to its cradle. Pausing, he rests his palm on the handle for a moment. His eyes focus on the framed American flag displayed on the wall. After a few blinks, his irises slide over to me. His eyes narrow briefly, as if a decision has locked into place in his mind.

"Sergeant," he begins. "I think it's time I brought my right-hand man up to speed." I square my shoulders, sitting up even straighter. I've reached a new level of trust.

Listening intently, I absorb every word he says.

Kuraly explains that unusual seismic activity has been recorded along the East Coast, in the Atlantic Ocean. Geographic experts believe an earthquake is inevitable. And based on the erratic readings they've captured, it's going to happen soon and it's going to be unlike anything this side of the country has experienced before.

Warnings blare through my thoughts, competing to drown out the general's words. *We've got to pinpoint an evacuation area and alert authorities. We'll need shelter and supplies ready to accommodate evacuees.*

He pauses, steepling his hands again, watching my reaction. He must sense that my thoughts are running wild. Recovering a slacked jaw, I swipe a poker face over my features.

"This, Sergeant, is what we're working toward. And our timeline was just pushed up." A smile crinkles the corners of his eyes, but frankly, the knowledge that disaster looms just out of striking distance does not warrant a smile. In silence, I wait for him to continue because his words suddenly make no sense.

"We're talking a major earthquake here—at least an 8.0. This situation is going to drive civilians to our installations along the East Coast. We've got to assume every base along the seaboard will be impacted. Estimates of the number of people that will be arriving are likely insufficient, just think of this as a pilot test. If we have that serum ready and a tracking system in place, we can start administering it to those who show up here seeking refuge."

My jaw twitches as I struggle to swallow the questions threatening to spill out. He takes that as an invitation to continue.

"We're going to help them, Sergeant. We're going to give them a safe place to stay. We're going to feed them and shelter them. And they're going to do one small thing for us. They're going to be injected and we're going to test Dr. Noori's tracking formula."

The marrow in my bones chills at his words. My gut tells me the doctor would despise hearing this called "her tracking formula," something she didn't invent, let alone the nano-technology that will accompany it, and I don't believe she ever would have. Like all of us, she's just following orders. Orders she questioned right from the start.

"When we reach a point of having to allocate resources, we'll know if this method is viable. And the beauty of it, Sergeant, is that the population at large won't even realize what we're doing." A satisfied smile washes over his face. Either he's completely fine with treating trusting civilians as guinea pigs or he truly believes this line of thought.

I stare in stunned silence, begging my chin to stay closed and my eyebrows to remain horizontal.

"Now, I'm sure you have work to do and I've got to check in with the team members who are securing additional food rations and supplies. This timeline impacts everyone." Clutching the envelope from Chara so tightly that my knuckles strain, I accept my dismissal and rush out the door. Besides the burden of additional work, the apprehension and guilt I feel from this newly gained knowledge weighs heavily.

Avoiding eye contact with anyone who happens to cross my path, I rush back to my office. They all go about their business of everyday life, with no idea what's coming. And it feels like a betrayal to know. I'm certain the general does not want me to share this information with anyone, not after how much he's stressed the confidentiality surrounding this initiative.

I spend the day forcing the big picture from my mind by consuming it with minute details of my tasks. I schedule my first meeting with Chara for tomorrow morning, knowing there's no time to waste. I'll spend tonight studying the folder he provided.

The evening's call with Rossana is brief. Somehow the information I withhold feels a little less like a betrayal if I say as little as possible. Every fiber of my being is screaming to warn her. I just need more time to process the information and find a secure way to communicate with her—a way not likely being monitored by anyone on base.

Chapter 14

After a restless night, I wake and ready myself for a meeting with the I.T. guy, Chara, at his office. Stepping through the entrance doors, just as I did the day before, sweeps me right back to the general's words, "unusual seismic activity along the East Coast…experts believe an earthquake is inevitable…if the serum is ready, we can use it on those who show up here seeking refuge."

I shake my head, as if clearing cobwebs from the corners. But the effort is meant to push the truth to the dark recesses of my mind. I'm still processing how to handle this new information. On the surface, I've been commanded, by a superior officer, to complete specific and immediate tasks. But on a deeper level, my conscience forbids compliance.

With my trusty manila folder in hand, along with a notebook, I reach his door. The gold nameplate confirms that it's the workspace of Brandon Chara, Division Information Officer. *I've come to the right place.*

The door is wide open, so I knock and step through the threshold to announce my presence. Behind the desk sits one of the tallest men I've ever met. He rises, thrusting his right hand my way for a proper introduction. *This guy must be at least six-foot-five.*

His dark hair is starting to thin in front and his grip is strong. His broad smile is genuinely welcoming as it reaches his green eyes.

After a few niceties, we get to work. I sit across from him at his desk, much like I have done with the general. The air in this space is much more relaxed, though. The walls are minimally decorated with a few framed military aircraft photos.

He turns his computer monitor so that it's centered between us. As he navigates to a database he'd like to demonstrate, I let my eyes wander the room, gleaning information about my new coworker from his surroundings.

His desk is orderly. A few framed family photos stare out from their positions on a bookshelf behind the desk. Each one captures three matching smiles in a flash of time. In one picture, they all wear matching yellow and black jerseys, clearly at a sporting event. In another, Chara and who I presume to be his wife swing a toddler between them, hovering the little guy's toes just above a crashing ocean wave. I can almost smell the sea air. *How many family moments just like this will be shattered when an unsuspecting earthquake wreaks havoc along the coastline?*

Sliding my glasses on, I track Chara's movement as he scrolls through screens, explaining functions and formulas behind a records system database he developed that is now used nationally. He whizzes through what data is collected and the various output reporting options.

When he finishes the mini-presentation, he watches me expectantly. "So, do you think something like this would meet your needs? It's just one option, but it could be a starting point for us."

I blow out a deep breath and admit my uncertainty. I reviewed his database specifications last night, but I'm not sure how everything will tie together. He closes out the file and folds his hands, resting them on the desk. Leaning slightly forward, he takes another approach.

"Why don't you tell me everything you need this database to do? General Kuraly gave me a vague overview but we should hash out details."

I'm walking a fine line here. I've got to give this guy enough information so that he can do his job, but I'm also expected to maintain confidentiality. Second-guessing every word choice, I tick off the list of data this thing needs to collect: basic identification information, and a unique ID number that can automatically, and instantly, cross-reference personal data devices. The only examples I can offer are fitness trackers, smart watches, and cell phones; since many people treat their phones like an extra appendage it's within arm's reach 24/7. And fitness trackers and watches are attached directly to an appendage. My assumption is that even if people found themselves in an emergency situation, they would keep those types of items in possession and make every effort to keep the phone charged. Unfortunately, I've been instructed to exploit the technology that could be a lifeline to their loved ones.

Like the database Chara showed me, whatever we develop will be used at installations along the East Coast and nationwide eventually. It's got to be compatible with all systems. And, it will require users to login so that we have a record of what staff members process which visitors.

Time passes quickly as we brainstorm options. My coworker eagerly ingests the database's requirements I provide based on the information I've been given thus far. He interjects solutions throughout the conversation.

Before I know it, early afternoon has arrived, and we never even stopped for lunch. When he suggests that we wrap up our discussion at the mess hall, I hesitantly agree. I could really go for a bite to eat, but the mess hall isn't exactly a confidential location to talk.

My gurgling stomach confirms that it's time for a food break. I gather the papers for my manila folder as he closes out of some programs he used as visual aids during our meeting then we stride out the door.

Chapter 15

We discuss immediate next steps in between gulping down burgers and fries. When Chara asks the dreaded question, "How quickly do you need this?" he practically chokes on a mouthful of food when he hears the answer.

"We pretty much have five days to get this operation up and running." I cringe as the words pass my lips.

"Damn, you're serious, Bowen?" he asks incredulously. "I mean, the general told me to make this my top priority, I just never thought it was *that* high of a priority." He washes down what almost caught in his throat and runs a hand through his hair. Taking a deep breath, his professional demeanor returns, washing over his features. "Well, I'd say we can definitely pull together a functional database and deploy it to the other bases rather quickly. I mean, with the general's support, that is. As long as word comes from him—and the sooner the better—I think the other installations can prepare by determining which personnel will be using the database so that we can quickly get them trained when it's ready to deploy."

I release a sigh internally. The general seems to genuinely enjoy talking about this initiative, thus I have no doubt that he'll be the one to announce the upcoming changes to the other installations. He probably already has a plan in place and I'm just not privy to it.

"No worries on that," I assure him. "I've got a meeting with the general this afternoon and I can certainly make that request." Chara nods slowly, running a palm over his face. Concern gnaws at my gut. I don't think I'm going to like his next words.

"So that is really no problem, but…I'm not so sure about the cross-referencing personal data devices," he adds. "I mean, I'm pretty sure it can be done, but the odds of it being actionable within a few days, along with the database…even if I work 24 hours a day, I need to reach contacts that won't be available at all hours. And I may need the general to make some calls to back me up."

"Understood. I'll discuss that with him today." Not much anyone can do if the tasks are too far-reaching for the timeframe. All I can do is alert the general. My appetite seems to dry up along with the conversation.

After we finish lunch, we part ways. With just about an hour until my next update meeting with the general, it's not worth trekking to my office without enough time to really accomplish anything. Instead, I walk. The movement wakes my cramped muscles.

Ignoring the stifling heat, I explore every vivid color bursting along the landscape—from the trees' emerald green leaves gently rustling in the humid breeze to the explosion of yellow and orange blooms among flowerbeds.

For the moment, I focus on the simple act of breathing and walking. I pass a dormitory-style building that is likely one of the barracks for privates. A small movie theater and commissary round out the structures along this path. As my meeting time draws closer, I stride past some residential streets and a playground. The slight wind carries high-pitched cries of joy as children soar down slides and glide forward and backward on swings.

I'd rather not witness any happy family moments right now. Besides reminding me of what I'm missing, it also provides an unwelcome glimpse of those who may suffer if this initiative transpires the way it's supposed to.

Although I arrive ten minutes early for my next meeting, it appears as though it's already started. The general's door is cracked open about an inch and voices carry through the gap. Unsure of what else to do, I wait. And listen. There's no chance I'm leaving and risking being late for the meeting. But I can't just barge in either. As I stand in indecisive silence, the conversation drifting into the hallway grows louder.

"Sir, I don't understand how I can test the carrier serum." I recognize Dr. Noori's clipped tone instantly. "Ideally, I could run animal tests, but there's no way I can secure a delivery and conduct testing within our timeframe. As far as human test subjects, I am not allowed to explain what it is, but I must run tests before I can verify that it will effectively carry and propel the nano-technology to lodge internally without causing any adverse effects."

I thought our status meetings were supposed to be for all three of us. I guess he's taken to one-on-one updates instead. Or maybe the doctor requested to speak to him privately. By the sound of this conversation, it hasn't just started. I'm guessing it'll wrap up in time for the next meeting, with me.

"As a matter of fact, doctor," Kuraly almost purrs, satisfaction dripping from each word. "just today we welcomed a group of soldiers fresh out of basic training. I'll make sure they visit the infirmary as part of their base orientation. Impeccable timing, if you ask me. You have your team ready for trials at 0700 hours in the morning. I will provide their superiors all the information needed. No one will question what you're doing. They will willingly accept the injection and offer you the chance to monitor and troubleshoot any adverse reactions."

A moment of tense silence hovers while the general's offer sends the hairs along the back of my neck to stand on end. *New recruits. They'll do whatever they're told, and they'll have no idea they're being used as guinea pigs.*

"Sir, part of my oath as a doctor is to uphold ethical standards. But one aspect of this assignment that I do not understand is where consent is requested. How can we begin to—"

"Leave that part to me," Kuraly cuts in, an edge of danger lacing his words. As if the brief response is half-statement, half-threat. I can only imagine the defeat Dr. Noori must feel.

"Sir?" the doctor says, a myriad of unspoken questions repressed in that one word.

"There's much work to be done, doctor," the general says

coldly. "You are dismissed."

The feet of her heavy chair screech along the polished floor, giving an audible sound to her internal protest.

"And, doctor?"

I inwardly cringe. Whatever the general's afterthought may be, it can't be good.

"I'd rather not use the term *technology* or *nano-technology* from here on out. Let's just say you're working on a serum. We both know what it will carry, so there's no need to repeat it."

Silence. She must nod or non-verbally acknowledge his request. *Maybe she can't bring herself to speak right now.*

I shuffle back from the door and stand tall, as if I wasn't just eavesdropping on a conversation that chills my bones.

The escalating cadence of boots clicking on the tiled floor announces Dr. Noori's appearance before she swings the door open and glides through the threshold. Her deep brown eyes catch mine and she slowly shakes her head. Without pause, she continues down the hallway, swiftly passing me.

Chapter 16

Partially stepping forward, I take the opportunity to knock on the general's door, even though it's now fully open. The general breathes out a sigh. "Sergeant Bowen, I see you're prompt as always. Please, have a seat."

As I slide into a burgundy leather chair, he sets the stage for the conversation he'd like to have.

"So, I'm assuming you've come to report some good news."

Now it's my turn to sigh. "Well, sir, I've got some good news and some…other news," I start. "I met with Chara this morning, and while he sees no issues with having the database complete and ready to send to the other bases within a few days, he's not certain he'll be able to incorporate the personal tracking device information into it."

The general rises so abruptly, I almost lose my train of thought. Clasping both hands together behind his back, he paces around the office. Eager to avoid what I expect to be an unpleasant response, I rush to fill the charged silence.

"He requested your support in obtaining what might be considered privileged information as well as your endorsement for when the database is shared across installations."

For a few tense seconds the only sound in the room is the general's boots clacking on the floor. I try to push thoughts of a circling shark out of my mind.

"Well, Sergeant, that makes perfect sense."

Wait, what? Is he serious, or is he just tempering a budding fury? Keeping my eyes fixed on the empty desk chair, I exercise my right to remain silent. It works.

"I am the official face of this initiative," he elaborates, continuing his walking tour of the room. "If any team members need a path to be cleared so they can complete their part, that is my role. Once he's got the bones of it together and can give me a concrete completion date, I will alert my counterparts at the other installations that will pilot test this along with us. We'll need to offer them virtual training and we've got to ensure that they are ready to hit the ground running when the time comes."

Okay, that went much more smoothly than I expected. For just a moment I forget the ultimate, dastardly goal I'm working toward.

"Although it would be ideal if the database could incorporate all of the information I'd like to collect as well as the information I'd like to cross reference, this is, in fact, a pilot test. We make it as accurate as possible in the timeframe we have. And then we improve the hell out of it."

The general finally ends his march around the room and lowers himself into his high-back chair. Sliding forward, with his elbows resting on the polished desk, his eyes hold mine.

"Think of it this way, you and Chara get me the database in five days. We deploy it. When he figures out how to add the personal device data, we release an update to the database. It'll take effect for all users instantly. Maybe it can even work retroactively, adding information for the people who were entered before the update took place."

"Yes, sir." I nod. Putting my moral conflicts with the assignment aside, this went better than expected.

"Anything else, Sergeant?" he asks.

"No, sir."

"Well, we've both got plenty to do. Relay my thoughts to Chara and we'll meet again at our usual time in the morning to review the status update."

I nod and rise from the stiff chair, content to be dismissed.

Trekking across base, I curse the searing heat that invites perspiration to itch along my hairline. It makes me crave Maryland's winter chill. Even then I like to keep the heat in the house at a solid sixty-four degrees. Rossana hates it. She's wrapped in a sweater the second the temperature drops below seventy.

I shake my head, refocusing on the present. The humidity felt at least tolerable on my earlier walk, and that wasn't very long ago. Turning my eyes upward, they rove the sky. Directly above, the blazing sun proudly blasts its rays through the atmosphere, but it's a completely different story in the distance.

Northward, somber puffy clouds loom. My guess is they're headed this way. Hopefully, I'll be back in my room before they descend and drench whatever lies beneath them. Picking up the pace, I arrive at my office, grateful for the glorious invention of air conditioning.

My first order of business is to call Chara and give him a quick update on my meeting with the general. His relief is palpable. It matches my own. He thanks me for serving as the go-between, acknowledging that the conversation could have gone south fast.

With that task completed, I dive into the other contacts I need to make. Before I know it, my stomach, not-so-subtly, reminds me that another mealtime is approaching. Packing up some work I can tackle back at my room, I brace for the heavy, humid air that hovers outside.

Instead of taking the time to sit and leisurely enjoy dinner at the chow hall, I grab a sandwich, chips, and a drink in passing and head straight to my room.

Chapter 17

After wolfing down dinner, I call Rossana. Her low-key day makes for a quick conversation. Instead of shooting photos on location, she spent the day in our home office, touching up photos and sending perfected versions to clients.

I talk about my walking excursion around base today but the descriptions in no way compare to the elaborate details she typically shares. Still, it feels good to provide at least some particulars about my day.

When the words dry up, we reluctantly say our goodbyes. I dig into my files and make notes of the tasks that must be tackled tomorrow. A few hours later, the crick in my neck serves as the first warning that it's time to shut down for the night. By the time my focus turns fuzzy, I decide to follow my body's lead, packing up my papers and readying for bed. Bidding my tactical flashlight and knife a good evening, I allow my body the rest it craves.

Morning comes too soon. I grab breakfast, then pound the pavement until I reach my office. I have just enough time to respond to the few emails that came in overnight and send out some high priority messages that can percolate in others' inboxes while I'm away from my desk. Before too long, it's time to return to the place where I'm becoming a regular: General Kuraly's office.

When I arrive, Dr. Noori is already waiting outside the door. She avoids eye contact. I follow suit. Guilt tinges in my gut. She's had reservations about this assignment since the first day and she tried to talk to me about it. I shut the conversation down, knowing full well we are not supposed to discuss any of this outside of official meetings. But now a nagging at the back of my mind wonders if things would be any different if she and I had that conversation.

Before I can dwell on any opportunities I may have missed to retain my conscience, General Kuraly's confident voice invites us to join him. I motion for the doctor to enter first. She deftly skirts past me and proceeds through the doorway to her usual seat. Before I'm completely lowered into mine, the general begins.

"Good morning." He eyes both of us impatiently, the greeting clearly forced. Resting on his elbows, he clasps his hands together and requests a status update from each of us. My tired mind wanders when the doctor gives her update. I try to focus, but she loses me after one too many medical terms: *adverse event, intradermal injection, allergens and anaphyl-something or other.*

The general strokes his chin as he listens, interjecting answers as well as counter-questions, along the way. When a moment of silence signals that the updates have been exhausted, he leans forward and shifts the conversation to his latest whim.

"Dr. Noori," Kuraly's eyes sweep over her as he gently taps the desk with his pointer finger, as if it's guiding his thought process. "I've been thinking, and I've come up with an added security measure that could greatly improve the whole formula." Her eyes slightly narrow but she says nothing. He continues.

"Let's say a soldier, or even a civilian for that matter, were injured. Let's just hypothesize that they were shot. If this tracker could lead us directly to them, we could recover our wounded comrade quickly and seek proper medical treatment immediately. This has the potential to save lives."

Why the hell is he still throwing curveballs at us when we have a plan in place and very little time to implement it? My thoughts race back to yesterday and my conversations with Chara, who looked mortified when I explained everything we were hoping to get out of this database. In T minus four days.

Strictly from a military perspective, what he's saying is true. And it makes sense in the field, in a combat or war zone. But once again, a major element is missing: choice. What he's proposing removes any possibility of knowledgeable consent.

While the overall strategy is impressive, the missing details percolate in my mind. We're going to use an imminent natural disaster as an excuse to test a tracking device on unknowing civilians. The serum will carry tracking technology into their bodies and any military installation with access to the database will be able to track their location and movement. All without their consent or knowledge.

Kuraly's right that this could provide an advantage in strategizing combat operations and the ability to locate any injured soldiers is beyond ideal. But so far there's been no discussion of offering it to any military personnel. And when we first started this task, the general stressed that we were working on an important initiative to help strike a balance between dwindling resources and a surging population.

When I read between the lines, I don't like what I see.

Chapter 18

Her deep brown eyes exude the exhaustion she must be feeling. I'd recognize it anywhere. By the end of each day, my own eyes probably mirror it.

"Sir, with all due respect, I am struggling to meet the deadline as it is. If we add another component to the formula, especially one that wasn't included in the original development, there is no chance I can have the finished serum ready for production in two days. Even if I were granted permission to add more staff to the team. It just wouldn't be enough at this point."

That's right. She needs time to fill syringes—maybe hundreds of them—with the serum and the device, as well as affix letter-number codes to each one so that we can cross-reference it during the intake process.

The general holds his palms up in mock surrender. "Message received, doctor." His gaze flicks my way, sending a wave of tension through me. "Well, as I recently discussed with Sergeant

Bowen, we're moving into the testing phase of this initiative. Once it's rolled out, we'll continue to enhance it. Consider the idea as the first improvement we'll make to the serum after its initial deployment."

Relaxing slightly, Dr. Noori nods. "Yes, sir."

"Limit initial serum production to two hundred syringes," the general states, narrowing his eyes and steepling his hands as thoughts pour from his mouth. "We'll ease the other bases into deployment after we have the enhanced formula. Maybe by that time, we'll also have the database cross-references added." He glances my way. I nod in acknowledgement. *Talk about a moving target.* Just days ago, he wanted every installation along the East Coast to inject people and record it. Now he's backing off until he gets his "improvements."

"Besides," he adds. "By that time, word will have spread around base about the new processes. While certain details of the initiative will remain confidential, we'll be able to allocate some medical staff to assist in syringe production so that we can properly accommodate the other bases."

I instantly wonder if this was the plan all along, but he didn't share it with us so that we'd push ourselves to accommodate his requests as quickly as possible. I'll never know because I'm sure as hell not going to ask.

"Well, then," General Kuraly states conclusively. "Sergeant, do you have any updates for me?" I shake my head.

"No, sir. I'll be meeting with Chara this afternoon for a demonstration of what he's created so far. I'll have more information for you in the morning."

"Unless either of you has anything else, this meeting is over."

I rush back to my office to accomplish as much as possible before lunch. The effort is largely futile. Snippets of conversation from the morning meeting waft through my mind, splintering my concentration—*we're moving into the testing phase...once it's rolled out, we'll continue to enhance it...*

Just how long will we continue to make enhancements? Because, I'm betting, I'll be here for each one. *How temporary of an assignment is this?*

With time constraints closing around me like moving walls, I wrap up just a few more tasks before leaving the solitude of my office once more. Factoring in half an hour to eat, I dash to the mess hall knowing I'll need to scarf down a quick lunch. It makes me wonder when, if ever, I'll have time to actually sit and leisurely enjoy a proper meal again. Lately my trips to the mess hall feel like a quick stop at a mini market, where I fill up with just enough fuel to last until the next stop.

A twinge of yearning flutters in my taste buds. The food here is good, I've got no complaints. But right now, there's an idle four-foot tall stainless-steel beauty just waiting for me back home. My four-burner Weber grill and I have created many a masterpiece together—from savory tuna steaks to sticky barbeque ribs to caramelized pear flat bread.

It's just one more thing to look forward to when this assignment is complete. If it's ever completed, that is. I manage to finish my lunch in record time and pound the pavement once again.

They probably should have just given me an office in the same building as Chara and Kuraly, given how much time I spend there. As I cross the threshold of the red brick structure,

I breathe a sigh of relief that this meeting is with Chara.

When I fill him in on the general's slightly relaxed stance on incorporating personal device data into the database, his shoulders instantly sag in relief. The knowledge renews his spirit and he enthusiastically demonstrates what he's already pulled together by way of a database so far.

By keeping the program at our installation initially, the pressure on him has significantly lifted and he promises to have everything ready for testing tomorrow afternoon. At least that news will make the general happy. I gulp down the extra saliva suddenly saturating my mouth. Knowing we're one step closer to making this initiative a reality threatens to coax today's lunch into making an unpleasant reappearance.

Chapter 19

The meeting ends on a high note as Chara's once again grateful for what he believes is my ability to broker a deal with the general. My new coworker is oblivious to my internal apprehension. I'm not about to say anything negative about my superior, and besides, I barely know Chara. He's a permanent fixture around here, and I'm just some temporary transplant.

My mind is numb from hours of discussing data fields, encryption, repositories, and information transfer. Perhaps consequently, my appetite is uncharacteristically AWOL. With no need for the mess hall, I stop by my office to grab some files to work on back at my room this evening.

As I sort and gather the dichotomy of scribbled notes and formal reports nestled in labeled folders, a blue sticky note flaps upward, drawing my attention. I don't even know where a supply of damn sticky notes is in this office. I've been limited to notebook paper.

Peeling it from the desk's surface, my eyes flick past the brief message. I know exactly who left it.

Please come see me When you have a moment.
— S

Before the glass doors slide completely open, the harsh scent of germ-decimating chemicals infiltrates my nose. *I'm in the right place.*

Approaching the information desk, I ask the attendant where I can find Dr. Noori. After a quick phone call, I'm directed to an office three floors above. One elevator ride later, I tread down a sterile-looking hallway following black arrows directing me from the stark white signs along the wall.

I hover just outside the open door, second-guessing my decision to comply with her request. As if sensing my presence, or likely able to predict how long it takes for a visitor to arrive after being announced from the information desk on the first floor, a voice calls out, "You are welcome to come in, Sergeant." Blowing out a breath, I brace myself for what I'm about to do.

"I am pleasantly surprised to see you, Sergeant." *That's not the greeting I expected. A simple hello would have sufficed.* I raise my right hand, flashing the folded sticky note. She nods, a tired smile cresting her lips.

"You are lucky you happened to catch me in my office. I am often on the floor seeing patients or tied up in meetings. Please, have a seat."

Right to the point. Can't say I blame her. I'm certainly not one for small talk, so her perception is correct in that I'm here because the words and thoughts soaring through my mind have to be shared. And no one else could truly understand the precipice I'm currently leaning over.

I scratch my head and shift my jaw, contemplating how to admit that she might have been right this whole time. With a sigh, I release the last bit of pride holding back my words.

"Look, Dr. Noori, I'm sorry that I wasn't very… approachable…when you tried to talk before." She holds my gaze, neither responding nor urging me to continue. I fill the silence by explaining what I'm sure she already knows. "We weren't supposed to discuss our assignments. And I'm not accustomed to disobeying a direct order."

"Please, call me Safiya." A brief smile flashes across her face to accompany the friendly gesture. It fades as her demeanor slightly shifts with her next words. "I understand, Sergeant. And based on your concerns, are you certain you should be here right now?"

I rake a hand through my hair and blow out a deep breath. First thing's first. I should return the gesture. "Call me Eric." I pause, glancing at the gray tiled floor. *Last chance to end this conversation.* No, I have to do it. Each day I march further into a battle that will have no victors. "Look, I finally see what you were trying to say. I didn't want to believe it. But the more Kuraly says, the less honorable this initiative sounds."

Whatever is going through her mind, I'm relieved that she doesn't respond with "*I told you so*" in a sing-song voice.

Safiya leans forward, pressing her hands flat on the desk, "I am relieved that someone else shares my concerns." Her eyes shift to the door, which I left open. I rise, quietly pulling it closed.

She relaxes slightly but holds her voice just above a whisper.

"But at the same time, I do not want to jeopardize your safety. And I believe that I'm being watched to ensure that I complete my assignment." Her eyes drop and she squeezes them shut for just a moment. "I do not know what will happen once the serum is deployed. It sickens me to know that it's inevitable. Whether I cooperate or not. If I'm not the one working on it, someone else will be forced to take my place." After exhaling a deep sigh, she adds, "And I do not wish that on anyone." I'm not sure if that part was meant for my ears but the tone is sincere.

Leveling a serious gaze at me, she shares, "I have noticed, very recently, that some of my…access…has been removed." I narrow my eyes in confusion, prompting her to elaborate.

"I can still conduct my day-to-day duties, but some of the information I had access to when we first started this special project—my 'permissions,' you could say—have been altered. It's as if, as soon as I complete a task, any record of the information I needed is erased."

"Maybe Kuraly's trying to remove any distractions so you can get back to overseeing the hospital." *Seconds after the words leave my mouth, I shake my head slowly. No, that doesn't sound right.*

With hushed voices and fast-flying words, we update each other on our individual progress. Our status meetings seem to have shifted. We alternate between meeting with Kuraly individually and together. We assume that Kuraly's keeping us apart intentionally, even though our work goes hand-in-hand.

After I finish, her eyes drop to the floor and her voice breaks. She struggles to form words as emotion tugs on each syllable. "I…I believe I've made a discovery about the nano-technology."

Leaning closer, I nod, silently encouraging her to continue. Her watery eyes search the ceiling as she lowers her voice to a faint whisper.

"I have access to a dummy database to test injection data entry. It is not final, of course, but it shows many fields that I imagine your intake team will use. When I cross-referenced the tracking devices with the test subjects, I noticed that there were additional options in the menu system. Options that require medical clearance, so that intake personnel would never see them. One of those options was 'End.'"

While Safiya speaks, I observe the details of her appearance. Exhaustion tugs at her eyes. A few gray hairs sprout from the otherwise smooth dark hair pulled into a tight bun. Any resemblance of a firm posture is gone; her slumped shoulders reveal a spirit struggling to stay afloat.

"What do you think it means?" I ask. *How the hell did Kuraly add features to the database without my knowledge? He must have worked with Chara directly.* I tamp down my anger with the intent to dissect this revelation later. I've got to focus on what she's telling me right now.

"I may be jumping to conclusions, but 'end of life' is the medical terminology for death. What if it's a way to activate the nano-tracker to end the life of its host?"

Removing my glasses, I pinch the bridge of my nose. *No. This can't be right.* She continues as my heart plummets and bile rises in my throat.

"I spoke to a friend at the Agency for Biological and Environmental Research. He's been studying biological anomalies in insects. His team believes pollution has changed their chemical makeup over time, enhancing their predatory characteristics and enabling them to inflict harm at unprecedented levels."

"But what's the connection?" I ask, my brain spinning on overload.

"This may be far-fetched, but…if the general's overall plan is to manage dwindling resources, what if that plan is based on something bigger than he's shared with us? What if this biological shift is a signal that we are on the cusp of facing an environment that grows more hostile and competitive for resources by the day?"

An ache awakens behind my temples. Too many thoughts race through my mind at once. I can't even formulate a response.

"If this started with genetic mutations—man-made if they're caused by pollutants—then we've got ourselves potentially hundreds of species of small, but amplified, enemies out there. There are already poisonous ants, hornets, and spiders, what's next?"

She pauses to take a breath.

"Now, add to that a slew of natural disasters, which most certainly will limit the food supply and access to basic necessities. If you were going to manage the population, in an environment that seems to be overtaking the human race, would you just stop at knowing where clusters of people are, or would you eliminate those that will eventually compete with you for resources?"

Chapter 20

Only a brief stop at the mess hall is necessary. My appetite is nearly nonexistent, but I'm not going to skip a meal just to wake up in the middle of the night famished. From the moment I left Dr. Noori's office, a haze clouded my mind. There's almost too much information to process and I have to wonder if we're missing part of the puzzle. Because the more I know, the more certain I am that this is wrong.

This whole situation is surreal. *What kind of government uses its soldiers and citizens as test subjects?* A strange faraway feeling overcomes me, as if every one of my senses is muted. Each bite of meatloaf lacks flavor, conversations drift around me but no words reach my ears, and even the overhead fluorescent lights appear dimmer than I remember.

Thankfully, my feet know the routine and carry me back to my room after I've cleared my half-empty tray. It's no lie when I admit to Rossana that it's been a mentally strenuous day. Concern underscores her words, but I remorsefully stress that I can't share details. Besides, I would love to believe that Dr. Noori's conclusion is wrong, yet I can't shake the feeling that she's cracked a code we didn't know existed.

My eyes drift closed and my imagination paints vivid images as Rossana rambles about her day. It's the perfect distraction, and exactly what I need right now. When our jobs take us away from each other, nightly conversations bridge the distance.

The telephone call provides a brief respite from reality. In one sense it ends too soon, because it leaves me alone with my thoughts, but on the other hand I'm more than ready for this day to end.

Mindlessly moving through the motions, I ready for bed. If only the next step was as easy. Instead, sleep hovers just out of reach. I lay still for hours, attempting to force my body into slumber. At some point, my persistence works, and I'm transported back to my younger years, when I'd first joined the military. Proud to serve my country, I had arrived at basic training ready to prove myself.

The stringent scent of the polished white tile floor permeates my nostrils. Perfectly spaced posters decorate the pistachio green walls—each featuring either a well-groomed saluting serviceman or woman or a middle-aged uniformed soldier, likely an officer, giving an enthusiastic thumbs up.

My eyes graze past the minimal décor and instead focus on the never-ending line I stand in. The view is the same in front and behind me—a row of at least twenty heads. From my vantage point, it looks like I'm in the middle.

Sporadically placed uniformed soldiers bark out instructions as the line shuffles forward. "Keep moving. An attendant will direct you to an open exam room when it becomes available."

Exam room, right. The dreaded trip to medical. Maintaining a confident appearance, I await my turn to be poked, prodded, and eventually given enough vaccinations that they alternate injecting both of my arms. No one asks what immunizations you've already had. Hell, they don't even tell you what they're giving you. You do what they say and then resume a place in the line so they can move on to the next person. Yet I sense no malice in their actions.

Next, I follow the snaking line to a large open room with twenty chairs aligned in five rows of four. All are filled with new recruits in various stages of hair removal. The constant buzz of clippers bounces off the walls, amplifying the sound. Between that and the flurry of activity, the room reminds me of an enormous beehive.

After shuttling through all the stops, we're escorted to the barracks and promised that we'll be given time to unpack belongings. But first, our new commanding officer strides through the door and introduces himself. He paces up and down each row of recruits, sputtering off expectations—ranging from personal hygiene to unit housekeeping.

The man exudes confidence and authority. His deep green eyes rove over each one of us, silently evaluating our reactions to the weight of his final message.

"I'd like to leave you with something to consider as you settle into your new quarters," he says, the deep timbre of his voice overtaking the sweeping silence. "When you walked through those doors today and took your oath, you became property of the U.S. Government. You will do as you're told, when you're told." He pauses, eyes drilling into each individual recruit. Just as he opens his mouth to speak again, I'm yanked from the scene, my mind

dragged through a hazy darkness.

The bleating alarm on my phone transports my muddled brain back to the present. The only clear thought I can process is a desire to be anywhere but here.

Chapter 21

My morning routine is a slow-go. Memories of my early days in the service awaken a nostalgic pride that I haven't felt in years. I've got no complaints about my home base or the work I do there, it's just grown stale over the years. Still, at this point, I'd give anything to return to that routine and leave this current mission behind.

I have no choice. I have to face the general and express my concerns. I'll never forgive myself if I silently comply with this manifesto. Besides, the general's easing Safiya's special assignment duties so she can return to her work at the hospital full time. Since I'm not stationed here normally, maybe he would take the same approach, turning over what's left of my tasks to one of his captains and sending me back to Fort Meade. In the time I've been here, I've readily accepted the work thrown my way and I'm willing to put in any extra hours necessary if it would shave time off my length of stay.

I swing by the mess hall for a quick breakfast and some harsh black coffee. Without even stopping at my office, I head directly to the general's building. While my gut twists with apprehension, my feet march forward. *I know what I have to do.* And I've got to do it fast before second thoughts force a retreat.

Pausing outside the general's office, I inhale a deep breath and square my shoulders. It's now or never. I rap on the door sharply. Kuraly responds with a half-grunt, half-greeting. With my chin held high, I pass through the door and smoothly pull it closed.

The general glances up from the stack of papers in his hands. "Sergeant Bowen," he greets me. "You're here early. Is there something I can do for you?" I don't like the hint of annoyance his words insinuate. Admittedly, he's a busy man and we have no scheduled appointment, especially first thing in the morning, but I've dedicated myself to a life of service. For the past two decades I've strived to be an exemplary soldier, accepting every assignment and deployment thrown my way. I've earned a few unplanned minutes of his time.

I lower myself into the chair and clasp my hands together. *Now or never.*

"Sir, I wanted to discuss some concerns I have about our current initiative." Carefully tapping the stack of papers before him into a clean pile, he rests it on the desk. Those pale blue eyes turn icy as they pierce my conscience. With every ounce of will I can muster, I straighten my back and hold his gaze.

"I just can't get past the lack of informed consent." *Oh, and the possibility that you're using the tracker as a weapon against your own people.* I rake a hand through my hair and elaborate. "I understand the value in this type of strategy, and in a war zone it makes complete sense. But what I don't understand is how we can justify testing it on civilians. At a time when they'll be coming to us for assistance."

The general stares in silence for a full minute. He's either contemplating a response or ensuring that I've expressed all that's on my mind. As time lapses, a charged weight coils around us. My gut churns as I anticipate his response. *What do I really expect him to say?* Something like, *"By all means, if you disagree with it, let's cease operations immediately!" is certainly not going to happen.*

Abruptly pushing back in his seat, the wooden legs screech in protest as they drag along the polished floor. Kuraly rises and clasps his hands behind his back as he paces across the office. Stopping before the framed American flag hanging on the wall, he speaks. His eyes remain fixed on the red-and-white stripes as intensity oozes from his low voice.

"That wife of yours. She didn't come with you to the base. And she never seems to visit either. Why is that, Sergeant?" He pivots toward me, narrowed eyes evaluating my reaction.

Dammit. Why did I come here? How could I believe that the person who's masterminding this whole plan would listen to an ethical dissent?

"Sir, her work keeps her busy and necessitates that she remains close to home," I say evenly.

Remaining in place, he nods, the slightest smirk playing across his lips. "You sure it's not because of that mutt?"

Damn him. Insulting my dog. That's a new low. I tamp down the rising fury, but it threatens to burst with every syllable he utters. "Well, sir, she really just can't get away from her job." I can't afford to take his bait. I've already gone too far and there's clearly no turning back now.

"Good enough," he says, turning away from me, clasping his hands behind his back again. He paces the perimeter of the room. Each step is carefully calculated, as if he's a shark circling prey, keeping a close watch while taking care not to trigger a startled escape. While I evaluate his body language, he artfully shifts the conversation.

"Sergeant, as you know, your work goes hand-in-hand with Dr. Noori's. And while she's more than capable of completing the task at hand, I'm sensing a bit of…resistance." He eyes me shrewdly. But again, if he's looking for some indication of my feelings, he's come to the wrong place. It drives my wife crazy, but masking emotions comes naturally to me. Although I don't respond, it's clear that I eagerly await every word he says.

"Anyway, there is a clear separation of duties, and while I initially thought it made sense for the two of you to meet regularly so that all three of us are updated on progress, we'll be curtailing those meetings. I'd hate to see any attitude of resistance rub off on you."

Possible responses flash through my mind. *Do I blindly agree with him?* It feels like the only option. Obviously, he doesn't want to hear my concerns or the doctor's. He wants them tossed in an incinerator and scorched to ashes, never to be heard again.

Silence is my only confidante now. There is no place for honesty or integrity in this conversation. His eyes narrow and his jaw clenches. I guess the only thing worse than disagreeing with him is not responding at all.

After a few quick strides toward the door, he squeezes the handle. Before twisting and yanking it open, he throws a few words over his shoulder. "Well, Sergeant, if you want to return to that happy little life that's waiting for you in Towson, you'll complete your mission and then forget it ever happened."

I don't answer but he clearly isn't waiting on one anyway. He pushes through the doorway, the steady clack of his perfectly polished shoes echoing down the hallway.

Chapter 22

I spend the rest of the day trying to push Kuraly's words out of my head. Why do the worst utterances always seem to claim prime real estate in our memories? Minutes slog by like hours.

Chara sends me a link to the database. Any temptation I have to question if Kuraly requested any features behind my back falls away with the growing realization that my actions will have real consequences.

I take the program for a spin, testing features and entering dummy data. Finding no issues, I congratulate my associate on a job well done, even though we've just scratched the surface of this aspect. While he tests the reporting options, I email the general, alerting him to the database's availability.

He responds almost immediately: confirming receipt of my message and that he will review the program and send me any necessary changes by morning. He also mentions that we should plan on training the staff members selected for intake duty tomorrow afternoon. The general promises I'll have that list in the morning so I can reach out to them with a time and location for their training. He's already alerted their supervisors, so clearing their schedules won't be a problem.

Just as I believe our correspondence will end without any further offense, Kuraly concludes his final response with a veiled warning: *"Glad to see continued progress. Keep it up so that we can avoid any potentially negative outcomes."*

My eyes jump to the framed photo of my family. A frozen moment of Rossana wrapping her arms around a vivacious dog that's half her size. No knife or tactical flashlight can protect against this threat.

A random person reading that part of the message could assume it refers to the direct task. But I know better.

I need to blow off steam. Postponing my evening visit to the mess hall, I make a beeline for my quarters, change into more appropriate attire, and hustle to the fitness center. Maybe if my body is as drained as my mind, I can just forget this day ever happened. Or at least the parts of it that won't stop replaying in my mind.

Fueled by fury, I scuttle onto a bench press, sliding my head and shoulders below the polished metal bar. Not even checking how heavy the circular discs balancing on each end weigh, I wrap my fingers around the thick rod. Lost in the repetitions, the surroundings fade, and pain invades my strained muscles. I welcome it, seeking a numbness that will encompass my whole being.

A white towel snaps in my peripheral vision, pulling me from the vacant nothingness the strenuous workout brings. Instinctively, I return the bar to its resting position on the uprights and search for the source of motion.

"Bowen, I didn't know you were such a powerhouse." Chara smirks, leaning against the bench press frame. Yanking the towel out of his hand, I swipe it over my face.

"Well, I didn't want to intimidate you. I mean, no more than I already do." I surprise myself with the quick-witted reply. Considering the day I've had, the brief exercise session has greatly boosted my mood.

He chuckles, running a hand over his face. "You definitely have. I'm honored just to be your towel boy."

Now it's my turn to chuckle. "I do appreciate it," I say. "And I'll be done here in a few minutes if you care to wipe down the machine for me too."

"As tempting as it sounds, I'll take a hard pass on that one." His smile and tone confirm he's game for the banter. He starts to turn away but hesitates for a moment, stepping toward me. "So, Bowen, can an old man like you still play ball?"

After a quick shower, I swing by the mess hall for some grub. Going to the fitness center was the best idea I had all day. I'm physically refreshed, and I may have moved beyond coworker status with Chara. Although socialization was never a priority for me on this temporary assignment, our brief encounter outside the office worked wonders to improve my mood.

In hindsight, all of my in-person interactions since I got here have been official business. My calls with Rossana alleviate stress and sustain our connection, but they don't last nearly long enough to rebuild the emotional well-being that Kuraly seems determined to extinguish.

I push thoughts of the general from my mind. He's taken up more than enough space there lately. Releasing a deep breath, I grab a tray and slide it down the cafeteria-style serving line.

Tonight's featured entrée is spaghetti and meatballs. Sounds good to me. I've actually worked up an appetite. Choosing an empty table, I consider Chara's invite.

He's part of a recreational baseball league on base. Teams are comprised of personnel from different units. The I.T. staff could use one more player on their team and he thought I'd fit in well, even for an "old man." Pffft…I've probably got five years on him, max.

As I twirl the long, saucy noodles around my fork, I second-guess my initial rejection of his offer. It's not like playing would prevent me from getting home sooner. It might make the time pass by faster. And it would be pretty manageable to fit practices and games into my schedule. Up until now, it's consisted of working, eating, calling home, and sleeping. A little exercise would do my mind and body some good. Besides, I get the sense that the longer I work with Kuraly, the more steam I'll need to blow off in the coming days.

Chapter 23

The surge of endorphins from my workout smooths away the jagged edges of the day. Talking to Rossana further pushes any residual frustration into the dark corners of my mind. I know it's temporary, but it feels good to forget about my reality and listen to hers for a bit.

Today she drove to Loch Raven Reservoir to snap pictures of the local wildlife and sunset. She left Millie at home in an attempt to gain a stealth advantage over any potential subjects she might encounter. Although the dog wasn't too happy, the decision paid off.

Sprawled out on the bed, I drape an arm over my eyes, blocking out the bland walls and harsh overhead light. *Damn, why didn't I switch the nightstand lamp on instead?* That dim bulb's the only one in this whole room that's not angled perfectly to cast a glare on my glasses. I slide them off and drop them on the pillow next to mine.

Finally situated with my senses essentially muted, I close my eyes and allow my mind to show me its rendition of what Rossana saw today. A box turtle creeping along the water's edge. Its deep brown shell in sharp contrast to the pattern of markings as bright as the sun. The cerulean-hued dragonfly with translucent wings in a variation of the same shade. No doubt Millie would have scared the turtle into hiding and the dragonfly never would have hovered close enough to be photographed.

When every detail has been shared, she asks about my day. Unwilling to relive the frustration, I skip over my encounter with Kuraly. She accepts, and probably expects, only minimal information. I rarely talk about work at home, and I'm less likely to talk about it when I'm stationed at another base.

I tell her about my trip to the fitness center and Chara's invite.

"That's great!" she exclaims. "I hope you're going to say yes."

"Well, I'm considering it." I hedge, not really looking for a debate.

"What's to consider? Besides, you'll probably only be able to play one or two games before you come home. You might as well enjoy it while you can."

Unwilling to share my spiking concern that this assignment isn't ending anytime soon, I mutter a simple, "Yeah."

"And I was thinking," she starts. "Maybe I should come down and visit you for the weekend. Since you haven't been able to come home yet. I can take Millie to my parents' house for a few days."

My closed eyes scrunch together but I'm able to restrain the sigh threatening to escape. As much as I'd love to see my wife in person, I'd rather she stay as far away from Kuraly as possible.

After his threat today, I don't want her anywhere near this place, even if it's on a weekend and the likelihood of running into him would be slim. My gut clenches just imagining the arrogant smile he'd launch my way if he realized she was on the premises.

"So…what do you think?" she prompts. The thoughts surging through my mind will not translate well into an acceptable response.

"I was planning to spend most of the weekend working. I figure, the more I can get done, the sooner I can come home." *How can she argue with that?*

She sighs, muttering, "Well, that hasn't seemed to help so far."

"I know, I know." *She's not wrong. But I'm also not about to admit that the general's been throwing changes at me that make it sound like this assignment will never end.* "And I'd give anything to see you, but let's wait a little longer and then hopefully I can see both of my girls…at home."

"Millie misses you." *Not as much as I miss that slobbering ball of fur.*

"Give her an extra squeeze for me." The tone has turned somber, and I don't have the mental energy to revive it. Small talk dwindles into goodbyes, plummeting my mood right back to the depressive depths of earlier today.

Chapter 24

Iwake the next morning with a driving motivation that my aching muscles can't hinder. The simple act of shaving makes my biceps scream with effort. I probably should have noted how much weight was on that bar yesterday before rage-lifting it.

After a quick breakfast scramble at the mess hall, I dive into a new priority, delaying my work to conduct some online research. Several clicks later, a bouquet of wildflowers in a green translucent vase is set to be delivered to Rossana this afternoon. The arrangement of yellow, purple, and pink petals surrounded by spiky blue bulbs will remind her that she's on my mind.

Pleased that my peace offering is scheduled to deploy, I reluctantly return to the task at hand. Almost immediately, distraction tugs at my thoughts. Motivation stalls as I consider whether there is truly an end in sight for this assignment. Dr. Noori's discovery of the 'End' command in the nanotech nags at me. Recent experience wrestles with assumption as my mind struggles to sort the myriad of uses that function could have, and why it was added without my knowledge.

Snippets of yesterday's conversation with Kuraly return, whispering in my mind, preventing me from crossing any items off my task-list. All too soon, the dreaded reminder pops up on my calendar. Time to face the boss.

Striding toward the general's office, I carry myself with the façade of confidence. My steps are fueled by frustration and my demeanor bathes in a forced projection of respect.

By some miracle, the final components of the intake process have come together. Kuraly congratulates me on accomplishing the task to his satisfaction, and in record time. My ears perk and my heart stutters when he mentions Lieutenant Colonel Morris, my direct supervisor at Fort Meade. Flashing a smile brimming with pride, he shares his intent to alert the man of my performance here.

It seems we're pretending that yesterday's discussion never happened. If only.

I shift in the chair uncomfortably. In the twelve years I've known Lieutenant Colonel Morris, he's demonstrated honor and integrity in his actions. And I don't like hearing his name pass over Kuraly's lips. Besides that, my home is in Maryland and Fort Meade is my home base. The last thing I want is for Kuraly to get any ideas about transferring me here so that I can spend the next several years under his thumb. He's definitely in a position to do so and my only escape would be when he retired.

My thoughts wander to what would have happened if

Lieutenant Colonel Morris had been assigned to this initiative instead of me. I imagine he'd share the same hesitations as me but somehow, I believe he'd have found a way to act upon them—sooner and more effectively. Before I can fully consider that thought, the heady silence quickly morphs into an awkward tension that can only be broken with a response.

Pushing past the discomfort, I answer as expected. "Thank you, sir."

Pleased with my reply, he slides a plain manila folder across the desk's smooth surface, depositing it in front of me. "Now Sergeant, your next step will be training." Nodding toward the folder, he continues. "This is a list of the intake team. These are the individuals who will be entrusted with following the documentation process. Everyone on base has a job to do, and this influx of civilians will increase their workload, but supervisors are preparing their teams. As of 1300 hours today, the intake team's schedules will be cleared, and they'll be all yours."

Great. On to the next responsibility. At least he's wasting no time.

"Sir, should I assume that the entrance point intake process will be part of this training?"

"Good question. I almost forgot to mention that I reviewed your report. Our onsite facilities team will take on that responsibility." His eyes sweep over me, awaiting a response. I'm just relieved it's not one more thing on my to-do list, but I certainly can't show that, so I remain silent. "They'll use the process you created. Fine work, indeed. You crossed every 't' and dotted every 'i.'"

I respond with a single nod but can't force another "thank you" out. The last thing I want to do is thank this man for forcing an immoral assignment on me. I take no pride in the role I played and would prefer to change the subject. The compliment emboldens me to ask the next question on my mind—where our responsibility ends and where other branches may assist with these efforts.

"Sir, is this team responsible for issuing warnings to the population at large regarding the seismic activity or would that be another entity? I'm assuming we'll coordinate with the National Guard." Typically, the National Guard is deployed to areas impacted by natural disasters, so I'm not clear why this mission fell to an Air Force base team. Unless Kuraly has that much power. This whole initiative seems to be his pet project.

The look he shoots my way warns that I've asked the wrong question. It was a legitimate inquiry. But apparently it should have remained unspoken.

"That is not your concern," he says, flatly. The finality of his words hang in the air like thick humidity just before a storm. Caution flares in my chest, but I can't stop myself. I have to know. "I'm anticipating questions when I train staff. They may ask when warnings will be released to the public."

"Sergeant, you're skating on ice right now. The thinnest." The general pounds a pointer finger on his desk's shiny surface. The thud echoes, his tapping growing more forceful with each word. "You will mention nothing about the earthquake. You will simply train these soldiers on a system that could be put into place at any moment when deemed necessary. But at this point *no one knows* exactly when that moment will occur."

His emphasis on the words *no one knows* is a direct message. Whatever he does know, he's not sharing. And that's truly the only way to ensure secrecy. Perhaps if I'd followed my orders without question, I'd know more right now. But just the thought makes my stomach churn with disgust.

Pressing those stubby fingers to his temples, his eyes drift closed briefly. His face clenches as if he's using every ounce of energy to restrain a pounding headache. Releasing a sigh, his hands still and his eyes zero in on mine. As he speaks, his pointer finger plunges to the table, solidifying the next words he utters.

"I need to know that you can set aside any misgivings you may have about this assignment in order to complete it."

His steely eyes study my every move. I force my jaw to unclench as my eyelids twitch. Although instinct implores my irises to examine the walls or floor or really anything other than the general's stark demeanor, I maintain a confident air in complete contrast of the turmoil raging within my soul.

"Sir, I will complete this assignment to the best of my ability." I force the words out, wondering what other possible choice I have. He's already threatened my wife and he could destroy my entire military career with one phone call. Would anyone else in my position give up everything to make a point? I can't win. Ethical dilemma or not, I have no authority or ability to stop any of this from happening.

He relaxes slightly, still watching me as if I'm a slab of meat on a grill just a few degrees between being undercooked and overcooked.

"That's good to hear, Sergeant. We'll touch base again tomorrow." With nothing else to say, the general dismisses me.

Chapter 25

The rest of the day and evening pass in a blur. Nothing matters now but getting home. That motivation fuels me to complete each task on my list. By the time morning emerges, I'm eager to prepare for the afternoon's staff training. My planning is minimal. Chara will attend to demonstrate the database, and I will present the intake process from entry to temporary housing assignment. I will not answer questions beyond those that apply directly to procedures.

A late afternoon appointment with General Kuraly pops up in my email. *Just what I need at the end of an already tiring day.*

I grab a quick lunch before arriving at the conference room early to set up. The training session goes smoothly. No one questions why this is suddenly happening. They simply accept a new duty at face value. It makes for an easy presentation, but it also makes me wonder how many other dubious assignments have gone unquestioned.

When the room clears, I thank Chara for his assistance. He shrugs off the appreciation, focusing on unplugging cords and packing up his laptop.

"So, have you thought about joining our baseball team? It's not too late." He casually asks, depressing the button to send the retractable white screen back to its resting place when not in use.

I'd actually forgotten about it until now. Maybe it's the need for social interaction or the temptation of forgetting about everything else in the world, but I surprise myself with an affirmative response. "Sure. I'll do it. Sounds like you need a secret weapon. It would be wrong to deny the team of my skills."

He chuckles. "Good. I'll email you the schedule. And I'll let you know when I have any updates ready to push out to the database." With that, he strides out of the room. My eyes follow his movement as a thought infiltrates the corners of my mind.

Chara's stationed here, so he's indirectly worked under the general for years. *Could he be unbiased if I expressed my concerns to him? Would he know if anything else questionable has happened under Kuraly's reign? As someone on the outskirts of this assignment, would Chara be appalled if he knew what was truly being instituted?*

It's something to consider, but until I'm sure I can trust him, it's probably best to stay quiet. That 'End' function didn't just show up on its own. It was an intentional addition to the program, one that I had no hand in.

Checking my watch, I have just enough time to drop some papers off at my office and catch up on any missed messages before meeting with the general. I'm certain he'll want to be apprised of how the training went. At least that's an easy update. I just never know what else he might throw my way.

When I arrive outside Kuraly's office, I'm surprised to see Safiya already there. These days I never know if the three of us are meeting or if it's just me in the hot seat. It's a relief to know I'm not going in alone this time.

We silently nod hellos. There's no way we'd exchange any damning admissions right outside the bear's den. Taking in my colleague's appearance, I feel underprepared. Her arms bear a three-inch thick binder organized by half a dozen colorful tabs dividing each section. A white rectangular bag dangles from the strap slung over her right shoulder.

At the top of the hour, the general swings his door open. He nods and motions for us to enter. As we take our usual seats across the desk from him, he asks for a status update from each of us. Fixing his eyes on me, I assume that I should go first. His features relax as I confirm that the training has been completed, it went smoothly, and Chara continues to work on the database enhancements that we discussed previously. Pride beams from his icy blue eyes.

They don't exude the same sentiment when they swing toward the doctor. Clearing her throat, she announces that she's finalized the carrier formula and that she has all the supplies on hand to move into production. Worry creases her forehead as her demeanor swings to concern.

"Testing has gone well. So far, I've not detected any adverse reactions. Granted, more test subjects would be ideal to garner more reliable results, but I am assuming we do not have any additional willing participants for further testing."

Kuraly's posture stiffens and his jaw ticks. Any relief I felt at giving an acceptable report sinks like a stone. I admire the doctor's honesty, but it's certainly not going to help her in this case. The room remains bathed in silence for only a few clipped seconds.

"Well," Kuraly starts, clasping his hands together. "It sounds like we need more test subjects. Dr. Noori, I assume you stand behind your work?" My lunch plummets to the pit of my stomach. *I don't like the sound of this.*

"Yes, sir, I do." She shifts uncomfortably, fully aware that nothing good is coming her way.

"Well then, let's give this a go. You can be our very first *willing* test subject." A sinister smile challenges her to decline. Closing her eyes and pursing her lips together, she nods. Hesitancy washes over her features. Clearly her hand is being forced but he doesn't care. The general wants what he wants and that's all that matters. I imagine this is punishment for challenging her role in this initiative.

What if I listened to her right from the start? If we both went over Kuraly's head, would things be any different right now? Probably not. His orders came directly from President Taves. *Who can override that?* Certainly not a couple of cogs with a moral compass that doesn't align with leadership.

I yank my sleeve up, past my bicep. "I'll do it. I'll be a test subject." I can't stand by and watch this happen. No one should be subjected to this without their consent. The consequences of what I'm about to do will have to wait. I'm tired of riding this yo-yo of right versus wrong, fear versus complacence.

Safiya's eyes pool with unshed anxiety. She shakes her head slowly and mutters softly. "No, it should be me. I did this."

"Sergeant…doctor, you both continue to surprise me."

Kuraly's clearly pleased with the path this conversation's taken. I once sought this man's respect. Now I struggle to choke back my desire to throttle him. "I appreciate your willingness to demonstrate commitment to this mission."

We both face him expectantly. For a fraction of a second my brain dares to question if he'll do the right thing and end this right here, right now. He rises, pushing up from the sweeping desk.

"Dr. Noori, I stand corrected. You are not our first willing test subject, but we still have one. Please vaccinate him."

She eyes me questioningly. There's no turning back now. I will not cower before this man. I will not beg for a different outcome. And I will not break rank. I hold the doctor's gaze and thrust my exposed arm toward her. "Do it."

I know she understands. She made the same oath to this country when she enlisted. The fact that she's still here, like me, means that she still believes in it. This goes beyond disagreeing with an order, but neither of us is willing to sacrifice our careers and our loved ones to take a stand.

With her eyes cast down, she unzips the rectangular bag at her feet. Slowly sliding slender fingers within the opening, she retrieves a single syringe.

With the smooth efficiency of a medical professional, she tugs protective gloves over her hands, removes the clear plastic cap, and plunges the one-inch needle into my muscle.

Chapter 26

Aslight burning sensation permeates the injection point, dissipating as the serum spreads. The pain is nothing compared to the guilt that slithers through my body, along with the tracking device swimming in the carrier formula. At that moment, allegiance unravels from my core to my extremities. The weight of its invisible fall crushing my spine as the burden of duty becomes unbearable.

All I've truly wanted since I arrived here was to complete my assignment and return home to Rossana and Millie. My behavior has put them at risk once again. Kuraly already knows where I live. He could find my family in a heartbeat if he wanted to. Now, even if I could get home and we tried to escape these circumstances, this tracker would lead him, or any of his designees, right to us.

I have little time to contemplate the long-term consequences of my actions.

"Dr. Noori, my initial thought was that you and your team would administer the tracking serum to every civilian that enters through our gates." *Could it be, does he see reason enough to discontinue this plan? If so, my sacrifice is worth it.* His cold blue eyes sweep across both of us, immediately chilling that thought.

"The more I consider this, it may be best to incorporate administration at the point of intake. The offices can easily be equipped with locking storage and disposal units. And this will allow documentation of the tracker number at the earliest possible moment. That would be more efficient for everyone involved."

He waves a hand around, motioning as he explains. "It ensures that no one passes through to housing without being injected. Otherwise, one could argue that if someone decided to bypass the hospital, we would have to cross-check every entry to ensure each person was, in fact, injected."

Nodding as his eyes focus somewhere in the distance, he concludes the thought. "Yes, we'll incorporate tracker injection with the intake process." He shifts focus back to us.

"Dr. Noori, I think Sergeant Bowen could use practice. After all, he'll be overseeing all of the intake procedures. Could you walk him through injecting someone? You readily volunteered and it doesn't seem difficult. Non-medical personnel could easily be shown how to take proper precautions as an addendum to their intake training."

"Yes, sir." Defeat resides in her large brown irises. I recognize the look because my eyes probably display a mirror image. *Dammit.* I volunteered to get injected and it didn't save her anyway. Honestly, Kuraly's probably just toying with us. He probably planned this all along.

Safiya explains the simple procedure. I hate to admit it, but Kuraly's right. It is straightforward enough that it doesn't require medical personnel. When she finishes explaining, Kuraly watches intently as I pull on gloves and select a syringe. I take my time, giving him the chance to change his mind about this, but of course he only offers encouragement to continue.

She releases a deep exhale as I plunge the needle into her exposed muscle. *Did I just sell my soul to the devil?*

"Sergeant, you have your first real data." Clearly pleased, Kuraly crosses his arms and raises his eyebrows. "I trust you and Chara can clear out any dummy information entered during training before entering your and Dr. Noori's ID numbers. It's time we get our data collection efforts started."

Defeated, I nod. "Yes, sir."

"General, I just want to remind you that, since we have limited testing data, we cannot accurately estimate the number of tracking devices that will fail. No matter how operational a product is, there will always be a percentage that are simply defective."

I perk up at Safiya's statement and my eyes shift to Kuraly. That bastard smiles.

He taps his pointer finger on the desk. "I agree that is a concern, doctor. But, hell, considering this is all a test that's been put on the fast track, all we can do is collect real-time data and adjust our methods as necessary."

Although she doesn't specifically say, I'm guessing this was her last-ditch effort to plant doubt in his mind that this plan should continue. It doesn't much matter if that was the case or not, because he's clearly not swayed. But if that was her intent, it demonstrates the level of integrity she possesses. Even when her superiors do not.

Silence indicates the meeting is over, but before Safiya and I can rise, the general's voice confirms we should remain planted in place.

Chapter 27

"One last thing," he adds. "We need to change our terminology. Serum was fine to use internally, when this was all just discussion, but now that it's becoming a reality, we need a more appropriate term. Serum sounds…like witchcraft or wizardry…or scientists in labs testing eye shadow on mice. We need to make this sound…beneficial…to those who receive it."

We sit in thoughtful silence, considering our options. I imagine Safiya's having the same conflict I am—there is nothing beneficial about this to the recipient, so how can we give it that sort of label? Besides, following the general's line of thought, perhaps serum *is* the right word. I mean, isn't that exactly what we're doing—forcing a test product on unknowing participants?

Kuraly plunks a stubby finger on the desk, rattling my nerves as I suppress jumping out of my seat. "I've got it. It's a vaccine. From here on out, we refer to this as a vaccine." He taps his chin, allowing his eyes to drift past our heads. "Now, what are we vaccinating for…" he mutters under his breath.

I'm no expert, but I'd say vaccines are meant to prevent sickness. They build immunity in our bodies. But from what Safiya's told me, there are no such properties in this formula.

Shifting those icy blue eyes between us, the general answers himself. "We'll be opening our doors to people from all walks of life, including those who are immunocompromised, whether they are very old or very young. And we are committed to protecting them from illness and infection while they are under our shelter. We all know how quickly a contagion can transfer from one person to another. Especially when an influx of people is confined within a space."

That would all sound honorable if there was an ounce of truth to it.

By the time I leave Kuraly's office, guilt and anxiety weigh heavy on my soul, tarnishing my mood. It's definitely time to call it a day. I swing by the mess hall and get my dinner to go. The isolation of my room offers a comfort that can't compare to the loneliness of sitting in a crowded cafeteria lost in one's bitter thoughts.

I force down half of my lasagna and garlic bread before calling home. Rossana senses my deflated spirit before I even finish saying hello. I attempt my usual distraction technique: asking about her day. She denies me that escape by turning the questions my way.

She knows I don't talk about work, but this time she deflects my resistance.

"Eric, what's going on down there? You haven't been yourself for weeks, but I let it go, figuring you were under a lot of stress." Concern coats her words. "But now…now you just sound…miserable. I know you try to hide it, but you just can't anymore."

"I'm really not permitted to talk about it," I answer. She deserves a better explanation, but Kuraly's words spring to mind: *The only person you may discuss this project with outside of meetings is me.*

Her rising frustration practically radiates through the connection. "Look, the longer you're there, the more distant you become. You don't want me to come down there and visit. And when I finally ask you to tell me what's going on, you can't talk about it?" she huffs. "What's going on, Eric? What's happening there?"

My heart seizes in my chest. *I don't want to put her in harm's way but how can I keep explaining away what's happening?*

"It's not you. I just want to make sure you and Millie are safe …" Sliding my glasses off, I squeeze my eyes shut and run a palm over my forehead. She waits. And she deserves to know. The sound clarity carries her nervous breaths directly to my ear. A tingle at the back of my neck warns me to lower my voice to a whisper.

"Look, this assignment, it's all wrong. Something's coming…a natural disaster is going to hit the East Coast and the government is keeping it a secret. They're going to open bases, but it gets worse—"

Even though she wasn't talking, I immediately sense emptiness on the other end. My words fade into the void.

"Rossana? You there?" Nothing. I disconnect and redial.

The damn phone's not working. I've got no reception, so I can't even text her. With the useless box of plastic, metal, and glass clutched in one hand, I barge into the hallway and rap on my neighbor's door. Other than the friendly nod we'll throw at each other in passing, we both keep to ourselves.

When no one answers, I pound on the door with slightly less vigor. Either he's not in there or he's ignoring me. Checking the phone again, I confirm it's still unresponsive. Moving on to the next door down, I repetitively strike it, allowing my waning patience to manifest itself.

The middle-aged bald resident swings the door open. I must have caught him coming out of the shower. Clad in only a stark white towel, I thank my lucky stars that it covers him from his waist to his knees. On top he's built like a bull. And he doesn't look happy to answer my interruption.

Chapter 28

Holding his gaze, I slowly lower my balled fist. No more need to knock.

"What's the emergency?" he asks, barely containing his annoyance. My own frustration fades as I reconsider my actions.

"Sorry to interrupt you. I was just wondering if you have phone service." His narrowed eyes convey what his mouth does not. *You banged on my door like the whole place was on fire just to ask about my phone?* His head twitches as if he's shaking away the disbelief.

I hold up my useless phone. "I completely lost my connection when I was talking to my wife and I'm trying to figure out if it was just my phone or if anyone else is experiencing it too."

"Which door's yours?" he asks. I'd really rather not share that information with a large man I've obviously angered. His arms are the size of tree trunks. I can't exactly just walk away, though. I initiated this conversation.

I point toward the entrance to my temporary home. "That one."

"Little busy right now but I'll check my phone *after* I finish my shower. I'll let you know."

"Thanks, and again, sorry to interrupt you." I shuffle back to my room in defeat. I have no way to contact my wife and paranoia courses through my veins. Did some cell tower malfunction disconnect us just as I was about to confess everything that's going on here? Or was our conversation severed intentionally?

I switch the TV on and lazily scroll through the channels, although no voices or faces drift into focus. The only voice I want to hear is unreachable. Alternating between checking the phone for service and staring at the smooth white ceiling, my eyes wander to the few stray cracks reaching from the corners. I nearly jump within reach of that ceiling when a sudden thudding erupts at my door. Okay, I see why my neighbor was aggravated when I practically assaulted his door, jarring him from a shower. *And at least I'm dressed.*

I jump from the bed and rush toward the noise. Sure enough, a fully clothed soldier stands on the other side. He wears an amused expression, which drops his intimidation factor down several notches.

"Hey, you're the one obsessed with your phone, right?" *Yes, that would be me.*

"It's not that I'm obsessed, I was just in the middle of a conversation with my wife. An important conversation…and the call just dropped. I guess I got a little bent out of shape." I rake a hand through my hair. This guy has no idea what I've been through since arriving here.

"Well, I just wanted to let you know that my cell phone's acting up too." He shrugs. "It's like it can't hold a signal. Never done that before." He shakes his head. "Anyway, I wouldn't worry about it too much. Probably just a tower down or something."

"Thanks for letting me know." He nods and turns away, definitively returning to whatever plans his evening holds.

Closing the door, I retreat back to my solitary surroundings. The paranoia diminishes slightly with my neighbor's confirmation that I'm not the only one unable to dial out. He's probably right. Whatever it is will be fixed by the morning. People can't live without their cell phones. If this service interruption is widespread, you can guarantee the carrier knows about it and is working to fix it.

Now, if only I could convince my gut to believe what my mind suspects.

Morning finally brings closure to an insufferable, restless night. A brief moment of hope flickers through me as I reach for my phone. This time it won't turn on at all. It takes about a minute for reason to breach the haze of my groggy brain. *Damn battery's probably dead.*

I trudge to my office, wondering how many more times I'll follow this path. At this point, I just want to talk to my wife. She *has* to know that my moods have nothing to do with her and everything to do with the crushing weight of this assignment.

As a thought tingles at the edges of my foggy brain, my feet pick up the pace. My cell phone may be useless, but the office phone hasn't let me down yet. Gaining momentum with each step, I struggle to maintain a professional image. A few passersby throw me questionable glances, but otherwise I focus on this immediate mission.

By the time I reach my office, I skid into the wheeled chair and unceremoniously glide to the phone. My fingers fumble over the numbers, misdialing several times. I hang up and inhale a few deep breaths, sliding my glasses off and squeezing my eyes shut. A few minutes later, convinced that I'm sufficiently calmed, I once again pick up the receiver, but this time carefully press the buttons.

Robotic ringing fills my ear, confirming that the house phone is working. My heart hammers. By the third ring, I'm choking back the words ready to spill from my mouth. The brief anticipation dissipates when the machine picks up. I audibly sigh as the recording of Rossana's voice instructs me to leave a message after the shrill beep.

I take advantage of the opportunity, reaffirming how much I miss her and how working here is taking its toll on me. There's not enough time to say much else. Besides, I'd much rather hear her voice than my own.

While my computer powers on, I pick up the phone one more time. Punching in Rossana's cell phone number, I accept defeat before the call even connects. As expected, it goes right to voicemail. It's nearly 0830 hours. She's probably out on assignment, which means her phone is muted so it doesn't startle any potential photo subjects.

I leave another message, knowing it will go unheard for hours. No matter. I can't delay the workday any further. Somehow, it's already time for another meeting with the general.

Chapter 29

As I approach the general's office, a silhouette slips through the doorway. Sure enough, I breach the threshold just as Safiya lowers herself into the same chair she always chooses. We share a conspiratorial glance. Age tugs at the corners of her eyes and any laugh lines that may have etched into her cheek have faded. I imagine my features have undergone similar changes since arriving here.

When we're both seated, General Kuraly announces that this is our last meeting together. Relief sputters but quickly dissolves when he explains that Dr. Noori's role is nearly complete. He has assembled a handpicked team that will oversee vaccine production so that she and the others who have been assisting her can return to their duties at the hospital full-time.

As soon as we have enough of a supply built up, we will deploy quantities to the other installations along the East

Coast. A member of the medical team will be given access to reports from the linked intake databases to ensure that vaccine production meets demand from all sites. He wants this to go large-scale as quickly as possible.

This act officially isolates me from one of the only lines of socialization I had. And that was really just to commiserate on our mutual aversion to this assignment. It's not like we went bowling or shot hoops together to blow off steam. We simply whispered about our shared concerns, knowing there was no alternative or escape. The reality of our nightmare peaked when we were forced to vaccinate each other with trackers. The resulting anger, frustration, and fear forged an unspoken understanding that no one else could understand.

"I believe that you are officially relieved of your special assignment duties, Dr. Noori." Kuraly rubs a hand across his chin. He's probably trying to hide the slight smile tugging at the corners of his mouth. Although that action would require a minimal level of decency that I don't believe he possesses.

Safiya glances back and forth between me and the general, uncertainty clouding her dark eyes. Kuraly offers guidance.

"The staff member overseeing vaccine production will reach out to you to tie up any loose ends. I appreciate the hard work and dedication you've put into this assignment and it will be noted in your files."

"Thank you, sir."

"You are dismissed, doctor." The finality of his tone propels her from the shiny leather seat. With a final nod, she grasps her folders and pen and slips out the door.

Alone with the general is one of the last places I'd like to be.

"Sergeant, you're probably wondering when your assignment will be complete." *Yeah, I've been wondering that for quite a while now.* He steeples his hands. "We're almost there. Just a few more items to cross off the old to-do list and you'll be on your way back to Maryland."

While I'd like to believe it, the churning in my gut warns me not to trust a word he says. Obviously, he has access to all the information he wants about me. He probably knows my favorite color is blue and that I was hit by a car when I was eight years old and spent three days in a coma. Still, hearing just the name of my home state pass his lips leaves me uneasy. I'd rather he just forgets that I ever existed. But I'm guessing that is too tall of an order now that I've got a tracking device inside me.

The general's next words yank me from my drifting thoughts.

"Next up, pack your things. You're moving to your new office." When I hold his gaze in confused silence, he elaborates. "You're heading up our intake team. That means you will be embedded with them in one of the intake offices. And besides, we need to free up as much space as we can."

Notes, phone calls, and checklists from my early days on base flood my memory. The trailers and supplies I ordered for temporary offices—one of those will now serve as my new desk and workspace. If only I could return to the familiar workspace I left behind a few hundred miles north of here.

He slides a paper across the desk. It slightly flutters before settling directly before me. "Here's the final layout of the new structures. I'd like you in Intake Office 3. Put your best soldiers in the first two offices. They should be able to take care of any unforeseen issues that arise. But if not, you're still available; you're just not on the front lines of the process."

I scratch my chin, scanning the layout. It doesn't vary greatly from what I had proposed before onsite staff relieved me of that duty.

"Reach out to the I.T. Department. Someone there can coordinate moving your equipment and ensuring that it works properly. As you know, the new office is fully furnished, so all you'll need to pack is your computer and any personal effects, which I imagine are minimal."

"That is correct, sir." *Other than the framed picture of Rossana and Millie, there's nothing here of sentimental value to me and I plan to keep it that way.*

"Very good. Well, that is all for today. I'd like to see you and your intake team up and running tomorrow, by 1000 hours."

"Yes, sir."

"Oh, and Sergeant, your focus is officially shifting. I want you to eat, breathe, and sleep the intake process. There's no need for further meetings with Dr. Noori or Chara. That will keep you free to focus on what's coming next."

Chapter 30

Since I'm already in the building, I decide to pay Chara a quick visit. Kuraly seems to think it's not necessary, but this is not an official meeting. It's just a convenient way to alert his department about relocating my computer.

His door's wide open, so I stroll just past the threshold and raise my knuckles, drumming three sharp knocks on the wood.

"Morning." I greet my coworker with a nod. He grunts in response, eyes glued to his screen. I guess someone woke up on the wrong side of the barracks this morning. Maybe I can lighten the mood.

"So what time's practice tonight?" I ask. If he's stressed about work or some personal issue, the best medicine is a little physical exertion. And maybe this will get him talking.

His green eyes widen with momentary surprise. Recovering, he slides his gaze right back to the screen. "Practice is cancelled for the rest of the week."

Message received. Clearly, he has no interest in conversation. I mutter "okay" under my breath.

When he makes no move to question why I'm here, I assume a professional demeanor. Stepping directly in front of his desk, I explain, "I need to move my computer from my current office to a new one. I can unplug everything and physically relocate it, but is there anything else I need to do? Does someone in I.T. need to flip any switches or connect anything? I have to be all set up by mid-morning tomorrow."

The seconds pass by at an achingly slow pace. His fingers tapping on the keyboard are the only sounds that cut through the awkward silence. Dreaded certainty grows in the pit of my stomach—I'd bet a month's pay that Kuraly is behind the sudden cold shoulder.

I thought this guy was becoming a friend. Had I confessed my doubts about the general, it probably would have been interpreted as disloyalty. I guess I saved my own ass this time by keeping quiet.

With his fingers hovering an inch above the keyboard, ready to return to their dance, he finally glances my way and blows out a deep breath. "I'll send someone over this afternoon. They'll disconnect and transport all of your hardware and hook everything up at the new desk. Just be prepared to be offline for a few hours."

"Thank you."

His lips twitch, as though he's about to say something more. Instead, his eyes slowly slide back to the screen and his mouth clamps shut. Without another word, I turn on my heel and retreat from where I'm obviously no longer welcome.

Fueled by frustration, I stride to the mess hall. *Will I ever enjoy a meal again?* Selecting an isolated table, I shovel in alternating bites of chicken fajitas and rice. This assignment can't end soon enough.

Rushing back to my office, I welcome the quiet isolation. I'm starting to feel like a twelve-point buck on the first day of hunting season. No matter what I do, a flashing target seems to materialize on my back.

When I'm knee-deep in responding to emails, a soft knock pulls my attention from the screen. A lanky soldier stands at the door, his thin fingers straightening from the fist hovered a few inches from the solid surface. The dark hair flanking his ears is starting to sprout patches of gray. He squints at the paper in his other hand and reads from it.

"I've got a work order here to move equipment for Sergeant Eric Bowen. Would that be you?"

"That would be me."

He nods immediately, relieved to be in the right place. "Is this an okay time?"

"Yes, just give me a minute to wrap up a message and close out."

"When you're done, go ahead and shut down," he says, stepping further into the space. "You might as well just call it a day then and show up at your new office tomorrow. I'll make sure everything's connected and working before I leave."

That last comment sends my thoughts back to Rossana. "Hey, do you happen to know if there've been any phone issues on base? I was on a call last night…on my cell phone…and the connection just dropped, and it hasn't worked since then."

"Not that I heard of, but speaking of that, your desk phone and email will likely work intermittently for the rest of the day as we reroute your extension. So that's another reason it's best to take the rest of the day off."

"Right. Thanks." I finish up and close out my screens. I quickly stack the folders and notebooks scattered across the desk and gather them in my arms, topping the pile with the picture of Rossana and Millie. Might as well deliver these to my new digs before checking out for the day.

Before I'm even out the door, the soldier reaches and contorts in various positions to unplug wires behind the monitor and under the desk. It feels strange to leave work early, especially when so much is going on, but it's not by choice.

Hiking across base, I locate the new intake offices easily. Dread invades every cell as I envision throngs of trusting souls passing through these doors, seeking refuge.

Chapter 31

Four mobile office trailers dwarf the landscape before me. The 60', double-wide behemoths are perfectly angled so that, if viewed from the sky, they'd form a pinwheel. That was part of the design to maximize the flow of foot traffic. While all four units will be used initially, the first two will process the most civilians, with the last two serving in an overflow capacity.

Gravelly paths connect each building to the next, extending around the perimeter. They snake through patches of upturned dirt scattered with grass seed and straw. Considering how quickly everything was thrown together, it doesn't look half bad. I shuffle up the squat metal steps. A black and white sign that simply states *Intake Office 3* peeks out from the window beside the stark white door.

I grasp the handle and enter my new space. Sweeping my eyes across the room, I absorb every detail. Privacy is a thing of the past with this set up. I've truly bid my private office farewell. *Hopefully, I won't be here that much longer anyway.*

Just a few steps past the entryway, two cramped offices have been carved out. A blue swivel chair sits at attention behind each metal desk. Stacks of folding chairs rest against the walls, ready to spring open when the need arises.

Striding past the initial area, a few cabinets and shelving units form a partial barrier from the next section of the unit. This part is a common area. Four cupboards hover over a narrow counter. It juts out, just big enough to hold a small coffee machine and the necessary provisions to brew steaming cups of caffeine. Next to that is a stainless-steel sink. A white compact refrigerator hums in the corner.

I peer around the shallow wall behind the counter. A basic restroom completes the other half of this space. I guess that's convenient. You can fill up and empty out within a few feet of each other.

Continuing forward, I follow the thin gray carpet trailing to the rear of the unit. The back end is a mirror image of the front: two metal desks, complete with a set of filing cabinets, shelves, and a printing station.

I stride back to the entrance to claim a workspace. Since the other desks are barren, I'm hoping the soldier bringing my computer figures out where to set it up. Dropping the file folders on the smooth surface, I gently place the framed photo of Rossana and Millie on top of them.

I have a feeling I'll be spending more than enough time here. At least my family will be with me, in one sense, providing a healthy distraction when my eyes can afford the respite.

With one last glance, I turn on my heel and retreat to my room.

I grab a to-go meal from the mess hall and bring it back to my chamber of isolation. It's best this way. I'd rather avoid running into the general or even Chara. To that point, I'm done going to the fitness center or really anywhere unless it's necessary to complete this assignment. Knowing that my every move could be monitored hinders any desire to offer a glimpse into my whereabouts. My sole intention is to wrap up the need for my services on this base. But even when I do head home, I know that my every move can be tracked.

By the time I finish eating, I realize that my phone's been silent all day. Rossana should have called me back by now. Unless she forgets, she typically turns the phone on and checks messages after she's finished a shoot and loaded the equipment in the car.

Other than a few specks of lint, fishing around my pockets turns up empty. I scan my quarters, investigating every surface. The damn phone is nowhere. It's not on the TV stand, the hotel-sized desk, either nightstand, or the bathroom counter. My space isn't exactly lavish, so there aren't many places for it to hide. Retracing my steps, I check every area from the front door to the farthest wall into the room.

It's gone. My damn phone is gone.

Chapter 32

Panic stretches to my core. Did I leave it somewhere or did someone take it? *Who would take my phone?* I should check everywhere I've been today. Maybe it's turned up in a Lost and Found box somewhere. Theft isn't common on a military base, which leads me to believe that if it was taken, it was an intentional, targeted act. My mind flashes back to the last conversation I had before my phone cut off.

I confessed to Rossana about an imminent natural disaster, and that the government was not warning people about it. Is it just coincidence that everything's turned to shit since then: my phone stopped working, Chara blew me off and essentially rescinded his invite to join the baseball team, and now my phone is missing.

Fueled by paranoia, I sweep through each room, searching for evidence that I'm being watched: a camera, recording device, or any indication that my actions are observed. Although I find nothing, my nearly manic state settles into a quiet certainty.

I will not find my phone even if I retrace every step I took today. I'm being isolated from every possible outlet until I comply and complete this mission. And even then, I could be recalled at any point, because I can be located with just a few taps on a keyboard.

With nothing left to give this day, I ready for bed and will my brain to take me somewhere far from here, to another time when conspiracy wasn't a part of my daily to-do list.

By the time my bleary eyes squint at the barking alarm clock, my middle-aged body feels like that of an 80-year-old. Or at least what I'd imagine an 80-year-old feels like. Or maybe someone who recently careened down a mountain. Slowed only by agonizing collisions with every raised tree root and stray rock jutting up along the path.

It takes every ounce of willpower my cramped muscles can conjure to rise from the bed. I shower and dress at a snail's pace. Envisioning the steaming cup of coffee awaiting me at the mess hall, I grab my keys and stumble toward the door. Before reaching for the handle, my muddied mind flashes a warning. *What am I forgetting?*

After a few-seconds' pause, my memory clicks into place. My phone. But it's not here. I'll check around today, but I have little confidence that it will make an appearance.

I skip over the breakfast offerings and instead fill the two tallest Styrofoam cups in the vicinity with coffee. Black. Nothing about this day will warrant the frivolity of sweetener or creamer. Trekking across base, I notice a few others making their way to the new intake offices. I recognize most of them from the training session earlier this week. I nod and flash a quick smile. These soldiers are following orders, just like me. The difference is, they have no idea just how wicked this work truly is.

Sure enough, my computer sits on the smooth metal desk I selected. My family stares at me from the framed photo atop the small stack of folders, just as I left it yesterday. At least that hasn't gone missing. Yet.

While the computer powers on, my eyes shift to the charcoal gray phone at the corner of my desk. I hastily grab the receiver, pressing it to my ear. My finger taps the keypad on the base, but nothing happens. Must not be activated, even though it's set up.

As my email inbox updates, a high priority message pops up on the screen. It's from the general, and he wants to see me immediately.

Chapter 33

Each step feels weighed down, as if my boots were dipped in concrete while I slept last night. Or maybe the mental dread has coalesced into physical reluctance. Either way, there's no choice in the matter. I stride across base to the general's office and rap on the door. Immediately he welcomes me in and motions for me to sit.

"I like you, Bowen." A churning sensation grinds in my gut. He rarely addresses me by my last name. It sends waves of discomfort up my spine. Smiling, he waggles a pointer finger my way as if we're old friends bantering about last night's game.

"I thought I saw a spark of disloyalty in you not so long ago. But I think I've managed to snuff it out." I carve a forced smile across my face. It brings to mind petrified wood—if I hold it in place long enough, it just may become permanent.

"No, sir," I force out. "I took an oath of enlistment and fully intend to serve that oath until I take my last breath."

He rises. I expect him to pace around the room but instead he approaches me and claps a strong hand around my shoulder, pride radiating from his pale blue eyes. When I first arrived here, I would have given anything to be in this moment. But now, I fight recoiling from his approval. A highly decorated general. The highest ranking official on this base.

"I'm glad to hear that, Sergeant. Because it's nearly time to put our plan into place." The words *"our plan"* send bile up my throat. Nothing about this situation was my idea.

"This seismic activity is expected to peak at 1000 hours tomorrow. The readings indicate this will be bigger than anything we've ever seen on the East Coast." He lets that information sink in before continuing.

"This evening I will alert all staff of the impending disaster. To alert them sooner could prompt them to share the information outside of this installation." Shifting into one of his signature moves, he clasps his hands behind his back and paces around the room.

Of course, it would. What person wouldn't call family and friends to warn them? *Well, I guess one without access to a phone.*

"I need you, and your intake team, to be prepared for civilians arriving as soon as tomorrow. The National Guard will be deployed to areas most impacted by the earthquake. Our primary focus is to coordinate civilian intake among the impacted installations. I've secured support from the Department of Operational Assets. We're on track to receive additional supplies and soldiers. This windfall will be split between us and our joint base, Eustis."

While I want to breathe out a deep sigh, I hold it in and

instead reply with my standard, "Yes, sir."

Narrowing his eyes, he faces me to ask, "Tell me, have you been assigned a cell phone since you arrived on base?"

"No, sir. I brought my own personal phone." I can't help when my eyebrows spring upwards with hope. That could solve my immediate issues.

He rubs his chin. "You know, on second thought, we should use walkie-talkies. It will give us a more immediate connection. Who knows what might get knocked out when this earthquake hits? With walkie-talkies, I'll have a better chance of reaching you. Actually, you'll need them for your team too. Since you're spread out among the offices and gates. I'll see that we get those today."

Anticipation deflates. "Yes, sir."

"Very well. I'll have equipment delivered to you. I expect you to keep it on your person or within arm's reach twenty-four hours a day. The outcome of this situation could very well warrant it."

I leave his office with my shoulders back and my head held high. Beneath the defeat, a tiny ember of resilience flares. I told him the truth. Just over twenty years ago, I swore to defend the Constitution of the United States against all enemies, foreign, and domestic. I swore that I would obey the orders of the President of the United States and the orders of the officers appointed over me.

But now those promises have become mutually exclusive. And if I can't do both, then I choose my country over domestic enemies that aim to defile it. Given everything I've learned over the past few weeks, I fully believe that to fulfill my oath, it means sabotaging this entire operation and the precedent it would set.

First, I need to ensure that my family is safe. And I'm certain that is of no concern to the general. Considering he's indirectly threatened them once already, I can't share this fear. Once my mind is eased of that concern, focus will shift to leveraging my position of trust to topple this initiative from the inside.

A renewed determination boils just under the surface of my obedient temperament. I'm not sure how and I'm not sure when, but I will have a hand in stopping this deception.

Chapter 34

That evening, at 2300 hours, the general's voice rings through the announcement system. Considering I've spent the evening in a perpetual state of dreaded anticipation, I'm neither surprised nor awakened by the interruption.

While some soldiers are working at that time since a base is a 24-hour operation, many are asleep. That was probably part of his plan. He waited until it was nearly the next day before sharing the warning.

"This is General David Kuraly. First off, I apologize for interrupting you at such a late hour. But I believe you'll understand why in a moment.

"It has come to my attention that the East Coast is on the verge of a natural disaster. And while this base is not believed to be in the immediate impact zone, we will be poised to assist those who are.

"We have been asked to open our doors to those who seek refuge. And we will do just that. A mass intake process has been put into place, although not for this specific purpose. It just happens to come at a time when we are more prepared than not."

Murmurs from the hallway drift to my ears. Human nature dictates commiseration to process this information. And my neighbors are no exception. There's only one person I want to speak to right now. She should be a simple phone call away but somehow that continues to evade me.

The voices outside my door grow louder as more neighbors congregate. I'm relieved to be alone in my room. It would have been difficult to swallow my disgust for the general's blatant lies. Somehow, I doubt my usual poker face could survive this speech.

"I am asking you to remain ready. Ready to assume additional duties. Ready to accept inevitable inconveniences that result from change. And ready to accept any order given. I will make further announcements as more information becomes available. Now, for those able, get some rest. I trust we will all need our strength and wits sharp over the next several weeks. I bid you a good evening."

Saturday morning arrives as a quiet hum reverberates across the base. Anticipation hangs heavy. For some, it's mere amusement. Not everyone believes that what is coming will truly amount to a natural disaster. For others, a wary belief shines in their eyes. Yet they remain the calm, confident soldiers they've been molded into. Tense silence hovers everywhere from the mess hall to the living quarters. The glaring humidity and fire in the sun's rays punctuate an already uncomfortable environment.

I follow the expected motions of the day, but below the surface, I'm an exposed frayed nerve. My external demeanor remains a collected facade. I haven't spoken to my wife in days, although it feels like months. My stops at various buildings: the reception area of Chara's and Kuraly's offices, the mess hall, and the fitness center have proven useless in locating my phone. And given what's about to come our way, I'm sure finding my cell phone isn't high on anyone's priority list.

I waver between a steely resolve to do whatever it takes to get home and a bottomless vat of guilt over what is to come. I hope and pray that my loved ones stay safe. And in the next thought I dread meeting families and other people's loved ones when they show up here under a false notion of security and protection. There's no outlet for my emotions, so I swallow them and simply proceed.

My role is to set an example. No matter what turmoil or fear rampages through me today, I will not show one shred of it. Whether this earthquake is mild or monstrous, my reaction will remain reserved.

By 0900 hours, the Intake Team assumes their positions, whether at the front gate, which has been retrofitted with additional security checkpoints, or in an Intake Office. And there, we wait. Pride washes through me as I observe the others, ready to face whatever fate brings.

Someone sets up a portable TV set in the trailer, readying for a stream of news once it's available. Bile hovers in the pit of my stomach, ready to rise, but just as natural as the physical response is a trained mental response. No matter what happens, every soldier on base has been taught how to remain calm in an emergency and how to mask fear. And today will be a test of that training. Not only for themselves, but in helping family members that live on base as well as the civilians we will welcome.

Just after 1000 hours, a low-pitched rumble greets our ears as the ground bellows and buckles, protesting the sudden shifts. Our trailer screeches, a metallic cry of shock and attempted self-preservation. Pens and staplers tumble off desks. Steaming cups of coffee relent to gravity's restless pull, staining the new carpet with soppy splashes. Wide-eyed, swimming in the surreal, we brace ourselves for nature's fury.

Clustering together near the door in case the earthquake necessitates a quick escape, my team and I randomly call out warnings and observations: "Look out, that printer's gonna fall!" "Hold on to something!" "Stay away from the windows!"

Our only goal is to remain calm while minimizing injuries and damage. Anxiety swims in my stomach as I envision all the people caught off guard by this event. We knew it was coming yet our complete lack of control over it is alarming. Mother Nature's in charge right now, and she doesn't appear willing to extend any mercy.

Chapter 35

A cacophony of sound surges, replacing the rumbling as it subsides. Car alarms blare, their screeching warning echoing in the distance. Voices rise both inside and outside the trailer.

The actual quake lasts only a few minutes, but remnants of its power are evident. Anyone who didn't believe Kuraly's warning needs no further proof.

I guess this walkie-talkie is handy. I radio my team leads, one in each Intake Office other than this one, to check their status. They all report the same thing: minor damage, no injuries. I instruct them to clean their area as best they can and ensure that it is safe for civilians to enter. As the lead in this office, I relay the message to my team as well. They set to work, returning office supplies to desktops, blotting spilled beverages, and restacking fallen folding chairs.

An announcement blares over the public address system: General Kuraly expresses his concern for every resident's safety and explains that an operations team is sweeping across base, assessing damage. Unless there is a medical or physical need, everyone should stay in place until they are accounted for by the operations team.

Other than being a bit shaken up, literally, we've been very lucky. My heart lurches at the thought of those who are truly suffering at this moment.

Within the hour, news channel helicopters deliver a tragic version of show and tell right to our screen. As time unfolds, the updates worsen. A record-setting 8.2 earthquake rocked the Atlantic Ocean. Delaware was hit the hardest, presumably the closest state to the epicenter. The earthquake threw Rhode Island, Connecticut, New Jersey, and Maryland into states of emergency as well.

Aerial views paint an unconscionable picture. We watch in stunned silence, unwilling to comprehend the devastation. Bridges crumbled like sandcastles on a windy day. Vehicles gridlocked like toppled dominoes. Billboards and signs plunged through cars and structures, unlucky victims that broke their mighty fall.

My hungry eyes devour every word and image flashed across the screen. I need to know if my family is okay. I watch intently, attempting to glean any assumption possible as to the likelihood that our home still stands. The information is too general to truly know how many have been impacted by the earthquake and to what extent.

I hover in a disoriented state, lost in thought, as my crew confirms our readiness to put all of our preparations into motion.

Survivors arrive before the day's end, seeking comfort and protection. Time passes in a whirlwind as faces and stories blend and mesh. No matter their physical appearance—gaunt, tear-stained, trembling—they all wear the same expression of disbelief and fear. Their weary eyes turn hopeful and relieved as they comprehend the sanctuary we offer.

Initially, I find some fulfillment in the comfort I can provide. Regardless of whether the government issued an advanced warning or not, people would still be in this predicament. Perhaps less people would be suffering less-severe circumstances, but no human created the earthquake. That's on Mother Nature. Acknowledging that fact helps me stave off the remorse of knowing that these people are truly being treated as test subjects in an experiment they know nothing about.

Within a few days, regret slowly creeps back to the forefront of my mind. Soldiers repair damage around base and welcome the temporary residents as best they can. The intake process runs smoothly, and Chara uploads updates to the database as he completes them—connecting cell phone and census data for a more comprehensive tracking ability.

The longer this goes on, the more mind-numbing it becomes. The worst part is making eye contact with people who are appreciative. They shake my hand and thank me just after I inject them with a serum containing invasive technology that may or may not be programmed to end their lives with the push of a button. I imagine if they knew the truth, I'd receive a swift uppercut coupled with some choice words, at the very least.

I'm starting to lose focus, not even sure what I'm working toward anymore. Who knows how many days have passed since I last heard Rossana's voice? My interactions gravitate around the general and waves of civilians. The former sends ripples of fury through me while the latter washes any remaining remnants of my conscience away.

Hope that I'll hear my wife's voice wanes. Cell phone towers have taken some nasty tumbles and power outages dominate pockets of the region. I know Maryland wasn't hit as hard as Delaware and our home isn't close to the shore, but I have no idea how she and Millie are faring.

Chapter 36

Time trudges like molasses yet passes by with chilling ease. No matter what personal anguish I endure, the days and duties continue. Each married couple I process shoots waves of jealousy to my core. They're in a lousy situation, but at least they're together. Negative thoughts fester into a downward spiral.

Each needle inserted into an unsuspecting adult or child strikes another gash to my morality. *I couldn't stop this.* And each person who comes here for help will pay the price. Willing or not, it makes no difference. There was never a choice. They may never know the level of intrusion inflicted on them—the result of seeking assistance from their government during a natural disaster, no less. Until it's too late. But once they've been injected, it's already too late.

Their movements will be tracked and, if deemed necessary, that information will be used to control their location. I'm certain the next step is going to be monitoring all those we've injected. Eventually, someone—and I can only hope I'm long gone by then—will control the division of resources.

The Intake Team grows more proficient each day, processing incoming civilians quickly and integrating them into temporary homes. The need for my leadership quietly fades, which should signal the end of my assignment.

But instead, it's as if my role shifts to a new phase. The general has unofficially designated me his go-to delegate when emergencies arise. I've acquired the role I sought in that first meeting with him: his right-hand man. And now I'd give up anything but my family to shed that role.

I'm the perfect candidate to handle whatever issue he chooses to pawn off on me. He sees my lack of nearby family as an advantage and uses it to call me over the walkie-talkie any time of day or night. It's become a lifeline that I'd prefer to sever.

The variety of tasks he assigns are probably meant to be busywork but are framed as concrete reasons to prolong my time here. By the second week after the earthquake, we are nearing capacity, which means general intake operations will cease and the team will be assigned population management tasks.

The general and I continue to meet regularly to discuss the evolving challenges of accommodating a large number of *guests* on base. While processes and procedures can be detailed and strategized, uncertainty prevails when you blend large groups of soldiers and those without a certain level of ingrained self-discipline. That very topic bubbles regularly in our discussions.

"Sergeant, I understand tensions around base are running high." General Kuraly's concerned tone catches me off guard.

Is he actually conscious of how this situation is impacting all the cogs *in his system?* Either way, I've observed the same thing, and I'm prepared to speak to it.

"Yes, sir, I've noticed a dip in morale and heard some complaints. Lines are longer at the mess hall, the fitness center is always crowded, and the overall noise and activity level has increased in common areas," I explain. "I know this has been an adjustment for the civilians, but our soldiers have also had to adjust to sharing everything from space to food to leisure equipment, and I believe it's wearing on them."

"Um hm," he nods. "As necessary as the influx of people on base is, I hate to disrupt our team. Without them, this place could never function as smoothly as it does." He rubs his stubble-free chin in thought.

"I agree, sir." He doesn't need my approval, but it's encouraging to know that he's both aware and concerned.

"Sergeant, I'd like you to keep a close eye on where disruptions happen most frequently. It sounds like you've already got a good handle on the various aspects of base life that have been impacted. Have a report to me by Monday with your recommendations how we can alleviate, or at the very least minimize, some of the stressors on our staff. Prioritize your ideas so that we know where to start as well as which recommendations are most feasible in a short turnaround time."

Every time I think my assignment is nearly complete, this guy finds another reason to keep me here longer. So far, I've struggled, but managed, to fulfill my duties with respect. But at this point my patience is teetering on a cliff of contempt.

Swallowing my preferred response, *Sure, I'd love to babysit civilians if it will make your life easier*, I simply reply with an affirmative, "Yes, sir."

His sharp nod confirms that I chose the right answer.

Chapter 37

As the unofficial base grievance collector, an influx of camouflaged bodies visits my desk. I document their issues and transform them into summarized reports to share with the general. His frustration seems to grow exponentially along with the complaints.

In a show of camaraderie, I make a point of following up with staff at their work locations. It also helps me observe exactly what they might be experiencing that's bothering them.

Trekking toward the front gate, rising voices draw my attention. I haven't even reached it yet and already tension is palpable. *Now what?*

A group of teenagers appears to be challenging a soldier. He's probably just explaining our admittance policy. Like it or not, it is what it is. Rubbing my temples, I pivot and stride in their direction. *No issues. No ruckus.* The last thing I need is Kuraly getting wind of this outburst.

Private Mitchell tenses when he notices me. I throw him a slight nod, silently dismissing him. I can deal with this. His tension melts, replaced by gratitude. He mutters as he marches past me. "Damn civvies."

"Is there a problem over here?" I ask. The tall kid with dark hair answers, "No problem at all, sir. Our friend here lost her sister and word is that she's on this base. So, maybe we could just take a little look around?"

Sure, go right ahead. Poke around under the beds and in the kitchen cabinets while you're at it too. Who do these kids think they are? Before I can shut down their request, another male in the group speaks.

"Evan? Or is it Ethan? Maybe Edward?" This moron thinks he can impress me by noticing the first initial on my name badge? I'm not in the mood for a guessing game.

"You may address me as Sergeant Bowen," I reply gruffly. "Follow me. We'll discuss this in private." I'm not having this discussion out here on display for everyone. I turn on my heel and lead them to my office. They follow in silence.

I motion for them to grab chairs and sit before settling into my own seat. As they explain why they're here, I silently evaluate their intentions. They appear to be telling the truth, but one clearly nurses an injured shoulder. No one mentions that.

Basically, they're here because one believes her sister recently came to the base. Against her will. The others were just along for the ride and are now hell-bent on getting out of here. This is the first group I'm aware of that's so eager to depart. Once we reached maximum capacity, we started sending civilians to our joint base, Eustis. They weren't exactly thrilled to be turned away.

I explain that they will all be processed, according to

procedure, and that the injured one will be required to visit the hospital before departing. She shyly thanks me. At least that isn't a fight.

Once they understand that they will get what they want—eventually—they cooperate. Except for one. Impatience radiates off her. Still, she'll have to wait. I process the other four and dismiss them.

As I give the group a few minutes to say goodbye to the one who's staying—temporarily—an idea surges through my mind. A dangerous idea. Her plan is to collect her sister and the two of them will leave, turning right back around and heading north to Pennsylvania.

In a cruel twist of irony, realization beckons. These kids can come and go freely, yet I'm here indefinitely, a prisoner of my dedication. My service.

An idea flutters through my mind, awakening a sliver of hope. The kind that can't be shut down without powering off the whole damn system because it's been running on back-up power for so long.

I shake my head and rub my temples. A chuckle slips out. *I've got exactly no other options. And if I don't do something soon, I'm gonna lose my damn mind. There's got to be a way to make this work. It's my only hope.*

After the departing kids all file out of the trailer, I return to the one who still has business here. Throwing the door open, I clear my throat. She eyes me warily as I cross the room and take a seat behind my desk.

She's quiet, but a growing impatience flares just below the surface. I sense a resilience that she demonstrated at the front gate. No matter what our soldiers said, this girl was getting into this base today to find her sister.

She's got fire. And feistiness. Sure to be a pain in the ass, but maybe, just maybe…As fast as my anticipation rises, the beginnings of a plan slide into place in my mind. I need to gather supplies and secure a vehicle. *This can benefit both of us.*

It's going to take fierce determination to complete this mission. And an unassuming appearance doesn't hurt. If she agrees to accept my proposal, the kid just might be my ticket to reaching Rossana.

AUTHOR NOTE

Dear Reader,

Sergeant Bowen's story was the hardest to write in this series. Besides being from a male's point of view, so many details required a lot of research—and pestering of friends and relatives who are or were in the military. I hope the result painted a clear picture of the sergeant's internal struggles as the story progressed, as well as what drove him to take such a risk relying on two teenagers to deliver a message to his wife.

This story was meant to provide readers with some behind-the-scenes information that Quinn, Riley, and the gang may never know. I hope you found it interesting and integral to the whole story.

If you've made it this far in the book, and the series, for that matter, please take a moment to post a rating or review on Goodreads and/or Amazon for each of my books that you've read. Reviews greatly help readers find books they'll enjoy, which greatly helps authors too!

Thanks for sticking with the gang through their journey and stay tuned for the series conclusion. *Hope Emerges*, book 5 of the Nature's Fury series, releasing in 2021.

In the meantime, I'd love for you to visit my website www.authoraefaulkner.com or connect with me on social media for updates and news.

ACKNOWLEDGEMENTS

Michelle Preast of Indie Book Cover Designs, this was by far the toughest cover to create in this series, but our efforts paid off! The images combine to perfectly portray Sergeant Bowen's internal conflict. Thank you for once again perfectly packaging my story!

Emily Angeline, Robin Asick and Beth Suit, thank you for your willingness to serve as beta readers! I'm always amazed by the questions you pose and the suggestions you offer—thoughts that never occurred to me, yet they make the overall story that much stronger. I really appreciate your willingness to accompany the gang on their journey, and you'll be the first to know when *Hope Emerges* is ready for you to wield your magic one more time.

Vanessa Anderson at Night Owl Freelance, thank you for your continued belief in this series! You've definitely motivated me to push this story further than I ever anticipated and deepen the characters' growth. Your input has resulted in crucial improvements that strengthen each book individually as well as the entire series as a whole!

Angie and Chris, once again thank you for answering my flurry of military base questions! I've referred back to your answers so many times as I was writing this book, and I am so grateful for your willingness to share your knowledge!

Uncle George, thank you for sharing your experiences at Langley AFB with me! I hope you recognize parts of the story that you inspired—such as Sergeant Bowen's flashback dream of

ACKNOWLEDGEMENTS

his first day in the service. I replayed your stories in my head as I was writing, and I hope I painted an accurate picture.

Rossana and Eric, thank you for answering my nearly non-stop questions about your couch, your dream job, what you like to grill…and so many more minute details of your lives! I honestly enjoyed asking you all those questions, and I hope it was fun for you to provide that input as well as read about your fictionalized selves.

Friends and family members, I can't express how much I appreciate your continued support. Thanks for sharing in the successes and excitement as I continue on this journey! And save space on your calendars until we can properly go on a book tour!

Scott, Landon and Aidan, thank you for being there before this series was dreamed up until now, when we're in the home stretch! Writing has taken a huge chunk of time, and I couldn't have come this far without you. ♥

ABOUT THE AUTHOR

A. E. Faulkner was born and raised in Pennsylvania. When she's not lost in a book, she loves spending time with her husband and two sons, especially while hiking, biking, or exploring nature. She loves *almost* everything about nature—ticks excluded, and one of her biggest fears is the repercussions we will face when nature can no longer tolerate human destruction. As such, she never tires of reading dystopian-themed tales. Stories about the end of the world absolutely fascinate her.

FOLLOW HER WORK

To learn more visit:
AuthorAEFaulkner.com

She can also be found:

Tweeting @AuthAEFaulkner

on Facebook @authaefaulkner

& on Instagram @authoraefaulkner

To leave a Goodreads review, please visit
Goodreads.com and search for
Allegiance Unravels by A. E. Faulkner.

HOPE
EMERGES
BOOK 5 OF THE NATURE'S FURY SERIES
Respect isn't always earned. Sometimes it's demanded.
A.E. FAULKNER